Reuniting
with the Cowboy

Shannon Taylor Vannatter

D0039616

 **HARLEQUIN** LOVE INSPIRED

Recycling programs
for this product may
not exist in your area.

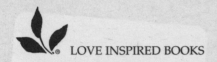

LOVE INSPIRED BOOKS

ISBN-13: 978-0-373-71977-8

Reuniting with the Cowboy

Copyright © 2016 by Shannon Taylor Vannatter

Printed in U.S.A.

Ally put her arm around Cody's waist. "Lean on me."

A bum leg was worth getting this close to Ally. He slipped his arm around her shoulders. Her fruity shampoo tickled his senses along with vanilla, and that fresh hay scent that had clung to her for as long as he could remember. The smell of Ally. He'd missed it.

"We're gonna turn around nice and slow and take you back inside. Once you're on solid ground, I'll go warm up the soup and bring it over."

"That's too much trouble." He really should tell her he could walk just fine. Just needed his cane and to take it slow. But what he ought to do and what he wanted to do were two entirely different things.

"No, it's not." She helped him climb his steps. "I won't have you hurting yourself for no reason."

She cared and smelled good. But he couldn't get used to leaning on Ally. Couldn't get too close. Not until he figured out his future. If he had one.

Shannon Taylor Vannatter is a stay-at-home mom/pastor's wife/award-winning author. She lives in a rural central-Arkansas community with a population of around one hundred, if you count a few cows. Contact her at shannonvannatter.com.

Books by Shannon Taylor Vannatter

Love Inspired

Texas Cowboys
Reuniting with the Cowboy

Love Inspired Heartsong Presents
Rodeo Ashes
Rodeo Regrets
Rodeo Queen
Rodeo Song
Rodeo Family
Rodeo Reunion

Visit the Author Profile page at Harlequin.com for more titles.

Commit to the Lord whatever you do,
and He will establish your plans.
—*Proverbs* 16:3

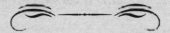

To Dr. Mark Baker, DVM,
for keeping my pets healthy and for sharing
his stories during our many appointments.
Especially the mad mama cow episode, which
inspired a fictionalized version for this book.

Acknowledgments

I appreciate former Aubrey City Hall secretary
Nancy Trammel-Downes; Aubrey Main Street
Committee member Deborah Goin;
Aubrey librarian Kathy Ramsey; Allison Leslie;
and Steve and Krys Murray, owners of
Moms on Main, for all their help and support.

Chapter One

Fifteen dogs and twenty-one cats. The number of strays changed daily—but one thing didn't—they all depended on Ally Curtis. This *had* to go well. She checked her appearance one more time, spritzed on vanilla body spray.

A clatter echoed through the house.

"Mom, you okay in there?"

"Just digging for a Pyrex lid."

Ally hurried to the kitchen. Her two Pomeranians trailed behind, their nails clicking across the hardwood floor.

"Found it." Mom snapped the blue lid onto a glass casserole dish on the counter. Layers of cream cheese and chocolate were visible through the sides. "I knew you'd be too tired to make anything after vaccinating all that cattle and we need to win over our new neighbor."

"You really didn't have to do this, but I'm glad you did." A cramp shot through Ally's shoulder and she massaged the aching spot. "Thanks, Mom."

Every muscle she owned ached as if she'd spent the first day of September steer wrestling. And she pretty much had.

Vaccination day at a large ranch paid a lot of bills at her vet clinic in tiny Aubrey, Texas. But she always came home exhausted and reeking like a stockyard. The shower had removed the stench but not the twinges.

At least she had another vet in her practice and the new tech she'd hired would relieve some of their load tomorrow. But it was only Thursday night. Two more workdays until her only day off.

"You smell much better," Mom teased.

"Definitely. Now all I have to do is lay on the charm."

"My persuasive daughter bearing a four-layer delight. Who could resist?" Mom's eyes widened. "What if our new neighbor is allergic to chocolate?"

"Or pecans." Ally's heart stammered. "Should I make something else?"

"Forget I said that." Mom winced. "If there are allergy issues, just apologize and I'll bake a pie or something else."

"If there's any more baking to be done, I'll do it." Ally picked up the dessert. "You've done enough."

"It probably won't be necessary. I've never met anyone who didn't love four-layer delight."

"Neither have I." It was Daddy's favorite. And Cody had practically begged for it.

Thoughts of her father always led to Cody. It had been twelve years since her policeman dad had died in the line of duty. Twelve years since her good friend Cody's comfort had turned into an earth-shattering kiss. A kiss that had dug an awkward gulf between them.

Since then, she'd seen him exactly twice. When their mutual friend married his brother a few years ago and when he was in rehab for an injured shoulder and knee after his recent bull wreck. Her heart had clamored both times. But his apparently hadn't.

She sighed. By now he was probably fully recovered and back on the circuit. Even if he gave up bull riding someday, he was a nomad. A confirmed bachelor, he'd never settle in Aubrey. And she was way too independent for anything other than friendship. *So stop thinking about him.*

"You look pretty without the braid for a change." Mom smoothed her hand over Ally's hair.

"Thanks."

"Want me to go with you?"

"Tempting." Ally took in a sharp breath and squared her sore shoulders. "But what if the new neighbor's not a people person? We don't want to overwhelm. All we need is some animal-hating grouch to complain and try to shut down my rescue program."

"We're probably overthinking the what-ifs." Mom patted her arm.

"I hope so." Her shoulders slumped. "I just can't believe somebody bought the place. I almost had the owner talked into selling me a parcel. Can you imagine how many more strays I could have housed with the extra land?"

"I'm sorry I sold our land off over the years." Mom sighed. "It should have been yours."

"Stop, Mom. You were a widow. You did what you had to do. We'll just have to make the best of it. If I can get on the new owner's good side, maybe I can eventually convince them to sell me an acre or two."

Two canine puffballs—one orange, one gray—danced for attention at her feet. "Poor babies. I promise we'll have a good long cuddle when I get back. But right now I have to go butter up our new neighbor."

"Rotten babies." Mom picked up a Pom in each arm. "You'd think they never get any attention. Despite these little distractions, I'll be praying."

A lot of good that would do. But she couldn't let Mom know she felt that way.

Ally stepped out and strolled casually toward the farmhouse next door.

She'd just wanted to be a vet, not run an animal shelter. Yet after a client had brought her an injured stray, word had gotten out. And before she knew it, Ally's Adopt-a-Pet was born.

But she was running out of room. Thank goodness the inspector had already come for the year. If the state showed up tonight, she'd get written up for being over her limit. All she could do now was sweet-talk her new neighbor. And hope whoever it was liked animals.

Trying not to let her nerves show, she unlatched the gate between the properties and stepped through.

The horse trailer by the barn had to mean something. Ally's heart rattled. Surely their new neighbor wouldn't mind a few dogs since he, she or they clearly liked horses. Surely.

A cacophony of barks and yips echoed from the barn behind her clinic. Her volunteers—three girls from the local youth group—strolled the property walking several of the dogs. She waved a greeting and climbed her neighbor's porch steps.

Who was she kidding? There were way more than a few dogs, with a generous sprinkling of cats, plus the pets she boarded for her traveling clients. And if she tried to shush the menagerie, it usually only made the racket worse.

Maybe she should wait until the teens left and the dogs settled down a bit.

The door swung open.

Cody Warren—in the flesh. Tall, muscular, with hair the smoky brown shade of a Weimaraner and soothing aloe eyes.

Ally gasped. Twelve years since his kiss had changed her world. Twelve years since he'd left to follow his dream.

Twelve years of trying to forget.

The glass dish slipped from her hand.

* * *

Cody grabbed the dish, his hands closing over hers. His breath caught.

Ally. On his porch.

Same old Ally. Long waves the color of a dark bay horse's coat, usually twined in a thick braid but loose today and spilling over her slender shoulders. Cautious coffee-colored eyes as skittish as a newborn colt.

He'd succumbed to her charms once. It had rearranged his insides and altered everything. Who would have thought one kiss would put the wariness in her eyes, build an uncomfortable wall between them and cause Ally to spend all that time since avoiding him? All because of his disobedient lips.

"Cody?" Her voice went up an octave. "You're my new neighbor?"

"Looks like." And now he'd gone and moved in next door to her. Maybe not the best way to keep his distance. "Let me take this." He scooped the dish out of her hands.

"I thought you'd be back on the circuit by now." Her gaze dropped to his shirt collar.

"I…um… I decided not to go back to the rodeo." More like his doctor decided for him. And that little bubble in his brain had something to say about it, too. "Aubrey is home and I needed a place of my own."

"You bought the place next to me?"

"This was the only land available with enough acreage to start a ranch." Technically leasing, with an option to buy. If he decided to have surgery. And lived.

She hugged herself. "What happened to Aubrey not being big enough for you?"

"Things change." A brain aneurysm changed lots of things. "Does your mom still live with you?"

"She does." She bit her lip. "Okay, yeah, I still live at

home. But it's the perfect place for my vet practice-slash-shelter and Mom's my office manager at the clinic."

"Come on in." He stepped aside, striving for casual, despite the drumming of his heart. "And tell me this is a pecan chocolate four-layer delight."

"It is. Mom made it, but I didn't come to stay." She glanced toward her place.

"You got a passel of kids waiting for you?"

"Um, no." Sarcasm laced her words. "Surely you know I'm not married."

"I meant the teenage girls out there walking dogs, but it looks like they're leaving."

"Oh." Pink tinged her cheeks. "They volunteer to make sure all of the animals get attention and exercise."

"Since they're leaving, I figure you can stay and help me eat this." He took her by the elbow and led her into the empty kitchen. Warmth swept through him. Shouldn't have touched her. Not even her elbow. "Come on. Humor me. Catch me up on Aubrey happenings."

"I don't know any." She slid her hands in her pockets. "I pretty much stay to myself except for cattle calls and hospital visits with my dog program. I hope the Realtor told you about my small-animal shelter before you moved in."

"Like a good Realtor, she did." He set the dish in the middle of the kitchen island and rubbed his hands together. "Actually, she didn't have much choice. All the critters were serenading us when we arrived."

"Do they bother you?" She grimaced. "The noise, I mean."

"Not at all. You know I've always been an animal lover. In fact, once I get settled in, I plan to come over and adopt a dog or two, maybe a cat or three for the barn."

"Really?" Excitement filled her eyes for the first time since he'd opened the door for her.

"Sure." Maybe the way to reclaim their easy friendship was through her animals. Ally had always had a soft spot for all four-legged creatures. He could lend a hand with the critters in her shelter. Maybe help her find homes for them. But more than anything, he could use a friend about now. He opened a drawer and remembered he hadn't even brought his utensils in yet.

"Why don't you have any furniture or appliances?" She strolled around the large kitchen.

"My home's been in the living quarters of my horse trailer for several years." Maybe he shouldn't have kept his move secret from his family. A furnished house might improve his rep. "I never needed furniture until now."

Over the years, his humor had pegged him as the class clown. His yearning for freedom and travel made everyone assume he had Peter Pan syndrome. His years on the circuit had only solidified his image as someone who refused to grow up, to take responsibility and settle down.

Now he was out to show everyone there was so much more to him. Maybe if he morphed into a mature adult before their eyes, they'd buy his cover. That he wanted to retire and be a rancher. Not that he was forced into retirement and might not live to tell about it.

"I'll be right back." He shut the drawer. "My silverware is still in the horse trailer."

"I have a better idea. Have you eaten supper?"

"Not yet." Why was she being so nice after making a career of avoiding him over the years? "But I can have dessert for supper." He gave her a sly grin. "I'm an adult."

"Jury's still out on that." She rolled her eyes.

Yep, he had a lot of convincing to do.

"Come on over and I'll warm up some taco soup." She scurried toward the door.

"You're making my mouth water. Lead the way." It

would be hard to keep up with her with his bad leg. But he didn't want to let on, so he followed her out. He'd made it down the steps and a few feet farther when he stepped in a hole and his knee wrenched before he caught himself.

"Whoa." Ally grabbed his arm. "Are you okay?"

Heat crept up his neck. "My doctor warned me to be careful on uneven surfaces. I've got a little hitch in my get-along these days."

"Why didn't you tell me to slow down?"

"I sort of forgot when you mentioned taco soup." Actually, he'd wanted to hide his weakness.

"How are you going to run a ranch when you can barely walk?"

"Easy. With a great foreman and trusty ranch hands. I'll be the brains behind the operation." He shot her a wink.

"Okay, change of plans." She put her arm around his waist. "Lean on me."

A bum leg was worth getting this close to Ally. He slipped his arm around her shoulders. Her fruity shampoo tickled his senses along with vanilla and that fresh hay scent that had clung to her for as long as he could remember. The smell of Ally. He'd missed it.

"We're gonna turn around nice and slow and take you back inside. Once you're on solid ground, I'll go warm up the soup and bring it over."

"That's too much trouble." He really should tell her he could walk just fine. Just needed to use his cane and take it slow. But what he ought to do and wanted to do were two entirely different things.

"No, it's not." She helped him climb his steps. "I won't have you hurting yourself for no reason."

She cared and smelled good. But he couldn't get used to leaning on Ally. Couldn't get too close. Not until he figured out his future. If he had one.

* * *

A waft of steam rose from the bowl of warmed soup on Cody's granite counter. Cody's counter. How had Ally gotten herself into this? She'd had a momentary lapse of judgment—that was how. But if the way to a man's heart was through his stomach, maybe the way to getting him to sell land was, too.

If only Mom could have brought the soup over. But by the time Ally got back to warm it, Mom had already showered and was in her pajamas.

As long as he'd been in the hospital and then rehab, Ally hadn't worried about him. But obviously, she hadn't realized how banged up he was. With him living next door and unable to walk across his own yard, he was like a magnet. Seeing him again, and seeing him in pain, had brought old feelings flooding back.

Staying away from Cody was the smart thing to do. But he could barely walk, much less cook. Especially with no appliances. He needed her help.

"So where have you been since you left the rehab center?" She leaned her hip against the breakfast bar.

"I stayed with Grandpa in Medina until this morning." He stood across the island from her, making quick work of the soup.

"Medina is almost a six-hour trip. You should be resting." She scanned the open floor plan, just to keep from looking at those mesmerizing eyes. Large roomy kitchen with a peninsula and a big eat-in area. The former owner had installed new cabinets and tiled floors a few years back, but Cody didn't have a stick of furniture. No pictures or personal items, nothing on the paneled walls. Not to mention necessities like a refrigerator. "Do you at least have a bed?"

"Grandpa sent one with me from his spare room until I get my own."

"So instead of resting in your borrowed bed—" she rolled her eyes "—you try and walk to my house on uneven ground after your doctor warned you to be careful? What were you thinking?"

"Taco soup." He grinned, deepening the cleft in his chin. "And four-layer delight."

Her heart did a flip. He seemed a bit more serious and mature than the Cody she'd always known. Until it came to food.

He wolfed down another spoonful of soup. "Mmm."

Gravel crunched in the drive and vehicle doors opened, then closed.

"Expecting company?"

"No one knows I'm here."

Ally peered between the miniblind slats. "A blue pickup."

"Oh no, they've found me." Cody hung his head.

"Who?" Ally frowned.

"My folks." His tone was filled with dread.

Why? He'd always had a great relationship with his family. Unless something had happened between them. "They didn't bring you home?"

"One of Grandpa's ranch hands was headed to Fort Worth to buy a bull. I hitched a ride with him."

"Why?"

"I don't want to be fussed over."

Audra Warren, Cody's mom, entered first without knocking. "Cody, what were you thinking?" She splayed her hands. "Grandpa said you came home to surprise us."

His dad, Wayne, followed. "We were worried when you didn't answer your cell."

"I forgot to charge it."

Despite Ally's attempt to blend into the corner, Audra noticed her. "Ally? How nice to see you."

"You, too." She waved her fingers.

"Why all the secrecy?" Audra's attention swung back to Cody. "We had to call the local Realtor to even find out where you were." Her eyes were teary, a testimony to a mother's love and worry over her recently injured son.

"I just didn't want a bunch of fuss." Cody hugged his mother, evidently feeling guilty now for upsetting her. "I'm pushing thirty—I don't need a lot of fanfare. And I figured y'all would insist I stay with you. I just wanted to come home. To a place of my own."

"We love you, Cody." Audra sniffled. "We merely want to help you get settled. But if you'd stay with us, we could at least gather the furniture we all have in storage and get this place livable for you."

"You should have called." Wayne's jaw tensed. "Your mother was worried sick."

"Sorry, Mom. I didn't mean to upset you."

"You don't even have a bed." Audra's voice cracked. "You can't stay here."

"That's the one thing I do have. I'm fine."

"I guess I should just be glad you're well enough to be home." Audra pushed away from him and gave Ally a quick hug. "Just like old times with you looking after Cody. Thanks for seeing to him."

"No problem." *Act natural.* She and Cody had been friends since grade school. That was all he was to her, a friend. "I brought a dessert to welcome my new neighbor, but once I saw it was Cody and he didn't even have a microwave, I brought soup over."

"Isn't this some setup?" Wayne winked at Ally. "You and Cody right next door to each other. Y'all could get into all kinds of mischief."

Like the mischief they'd gotten into twelve years ago. No way. Ally's lips would steer clear of Cody Warren this go-round.

In fact, all of her would. "Since y'all are here, I'm gonna go."

Cody grabbed her hand. "I wish you'd stay. We've still got catching up to do."

Electricity moved up her arm. Ally pulled away. "I've got chores to do and a surgery in the morning. It's good seeing y'all." She aimed for the door and put it in high gear.

Distance. She'd have to keep lots of distance between her and Cody. Her heart couldn't take any more teasing.

Cody scanned his cozy house, grateful to have a loving family. Even though they sometimes smothered him.

Only twenty-four hours since his parents had caught up with him and his new house was already furnished. There would have been even more fuss if he'd told his family he was leaving Grandpa's. And if he'd accepted a ride *home* from his parents, he'd have likely ended up at their house. Yet because of them, he actually had a table to sit at to savor his last serving of four-layer delight.

In a day's time, his dad and his brother, Mitch, had brought over Mitch's old dining room set, appliances and dual recliner couch, along with Cody's old bedroom suite from when he lived at home. He'd moved out twelve years ago and Mitch had given up his bachelor pad two years ago, but they had kept everything. His family officially ranked as hoarders.

The rich coffee aroma still permeated his house, as they'd offered him countless cups throughout the day.

If only he could have the real stuff instead of the fake. The empty maker mocked him from the counter. He'd die for a cup. Literally. He filled the carafe with water, poured it in the back, scooped decaf grounds into the filter and turned it on. It would have to do.

The doctor's list of aneurysm triggers included intense nose blowing, vigorous exercise and strain. Since he had no allergies, he should be okay unless he got a cold.

It was a genuine wonder the aneurysm hadn't ruptured during his physical therapy, which came to a screeching halt after his doctor found the bubble during a follow up scan after his last concussion. Hopefully, his leisurely walks on his new treadmill would help with his limp.

Anger and surprise would be easy to avoid since he was laid-back and not easily startled. But real coffee? He came from a family that joked about having caffeine in their veins instead of blood. Having his dark roast again just might be worth the surgery that could kill him or reduce him to vegetable status.

He scraped all the excess chocolate and crumbs out of the glass dish and polished off the last bite of the lipsmacking dessert. The tang of cream cheese lingered on his tongue.

Despite all the activity and furnishings, Ally had stayed away. Her mom had brought him a casserole, but he hadn't seen hide nor hair of Ally since yesterday.

Maybe moving next door to her hadn't been the best plan. It was the only land he'd found to lease, but it wasn't a good way to relieve the tension between them and get their friendship back on track.

He stood and waited until the stiffness eased in his knee before shuffling to the sink, then made short work of washing the pan and poured a cup of decaf.

Since they'd grown up in the same church, hung out in youth group and been in the same class, he, Ally and his now-sister-in-law, Caitlyn, had been best friends all the way back to kindergarten.

But Ally had avoided him at Mitch and Caitlyn's wedding. And after his bull wreck, when Ally had visited the rehab center with her dog program and had realized her patient was him, she hadn't been able to get out of there fast enough.

She was obviously uncomfortable because of that kiss that had spun his world into a blur faster than any bull ever had.

But hadn't affected her.

Maybe they needed to talk about the kiss. Agree to forget it. He dried the glass dish and tucked it under his arm. If he walked slow and careful and took the stupid stick, he could handle the uneven yard. He gulped the useless coffee, grabbed the cane and stepped out his back door.

Must have been after hours for her clinic. Only one other truck and a car were parked next to Ally's—probably one of her youth group volunteers. He continued past the house to the block structure with a neon open sign in the window.

A cowbell clanged when he opened the door.

"I'll be right with you," Ally called from the back. "Is it an emergency?"

"It's just me."

Silence.

A deep woof came from behind the counter. Cody eased closer. A male German shepherd lay sprawled on the floor, his ears perked up.

"Hey, buddy, don't worry—the vet's nice." He lowered his voice. "And she's a looker, too."

He set the dish on the counter, settled in a chair in the waiting area, picked up a livestock magazine and thumbed through it.

"You know I'm on your side, Ms. Curtis." A man's voice came from the back. "I love animals as much as you do.

But you're not in compliance with the cats. You're supposed to provide eighteen square feet per cat."

"The mama cat and two kittens just came in yesterday." Her words came fast, desperate. "Their owners moved and abandoned them. I just couldn't turn them away. I planned to buy some more acreage so I could expand, but someone else beat me to the property."

He'd tied up the land she needed. Cody closed his eyes.

"I'm sorry, but I'll have to write you up."

A pause.

"I understand." She sounded so broken.

And now she was in trouble.

Cody had to find a way to fix it.

Chapter Two

"**M**aybe you should consider revoking your no-kill policy." Mr. Humphries wouldn't even look at her as he flipped to the appropriate form on his clipboard.

"I can't do that." Ally's heart squeezed. Kill a perfectly healthy animal just because no one wanted it?

"You know I'm against it, too. Maybe you could take some of the cats to another shelter."

A lump lodged in her throat. "So they can put them down?"

"I'm sorry, Ms. Curtis." The inspector strolled toward the front of her clinic.

Come on—think of some way to change his mind. Ally hurried after him.

"Excuse me." Cody met them in the lobby, removed his cowboy hat. "I came to pick out those cats we talked about."

Mr. Humphries's eyes narrowed with suspicion.

Ally's insides lit up. "How many would you like?" She held up three fingers behind Mr. Humphries's back.

"Four."

"Four?" Mr. Humphries echoed.

Four? Her heart warmed.

"Just moved in next door. Cody Warren." He offered his hand and the older man shook it. "My barn is infested with mice. I'm thinking four cats should take care of the problem."

He sounded so convincing she wanted to hug him.

Mr. Humphries examined Cody a moment longer, then turned to Ally. "You run a clean operation here." He slid his pen into his pocket, tucked the clipboard under his arm. "I don't want to have to shut you down. See that you stay in compliance. I doubt that your neighbor can rescue you next time."

"Thank you, Mr. Humphries."

"And I trust—" he gave her a stern look "—that if I come back in an hour, you'll be down three cats."

"Four and they'll be in my barn." Cody clasped his hat to his chest. "You're welcome to come visit them."

With a slight nod, the inspector exited the clinic.

Ally waited, held her breath. A car door shut and an engine started. "Thank you, thank you, thank you." She jumped up and down.

"Just call me Ally's hero." He shot her a wink that made her heart take a dive.

Her fists clenched. Now he wanted to be her hero?

"You should have told me you were over the limit. I'd have taken the cats before your inspector came."

"It's really weird." She nibbled the inside of her cheek. "I've already been inspected for this year. Someone had to complain for Mr. Humphries to show up again."

"Who would do that? We don't have any other neighbors."

"I don't know, unless it was a client." She twirled the end of her braid round and round her finger the way her dad used to do. "I've had a few new ones lately. Maybe someone didn't like what they saw." Not everyone liked her strays or her shelter. Some people could be so heartless.

"If that's the case, they should find another vet instead of hassling you." He gestured to the shepherd. "What's he in for? Armed doggery?"

She suppressed a grin. "Hoss is just staying with me while his family is on vacation. I didn't have time to put him in a run yet." The dog's tail wagged as she snapped a leash on his collar. "Why did you really stop by?"

"I brought your dish back. All washed and everything."

"You didn't have to do that." She raised an eyebrow. "You walked across my rutted yard for that?"

"I took it slow with my trusty stick." He patted his cane, cleared his throat. "I also wanted to discuss…uh…to ask you for contacts on some hands. Since you do cattle vaccinations, I figured you'd know the right people."

Nervous? Cody Warren nervous? About asking her for ranch hand contacts? She strode over to the bulletin board.

"A large ranch in the area just downsized. Lots of lay-offs." She removed a business card and pulled two stubs bearing names and numbers, then passed them to him. "The card is the ranch owner for references. The numbers are hands." She rubbed the ache in the back of her neck.

"All your tension still lands in your neck and shoulders, huh?" Cody stuffed the contacts in his shirt pocket and limped around behind her. His warm hands grasped her shoulders, kneading her sore muscles.

She stiffened, almost pulled away. But when she began to relax, all thought of getting away left her. She had to focus on something other than the shivers he was stirring up. "I won't hold you to four cats. If you'll just take three, I'll be under limit."

"I want four. I was thinking I'd take the ones who've been here longest. But it would be a shame to separate the mama and her kittens, so I'll take those three plus one of the veterans."

Such a sweetheart. Not many men thought that way. If he ever grew up and settled down, he'd make someone a great husband. "That would be Bruno. His past shouldn't be a problem."

"You know his story?" His thumbs soothed away her aches.

What was she talking about? Oh yes, Bruno. "He killed his former neighbor's pet rabbit and chickens. We don't have any of either near here and he won't be wandering far from home anymore since I neutered him."

"Hear that, Hoss." The German shepherd's ears pricked. "You better stay on her good side."

"I need to get him in his run." She stiffened again, pulled away and dug four collapsed cardboard carriers from under the counter. "And we better go get the cats before Mr. Humphries decides to come back."

And before she melted into a pool of butter at Cody's feet.

Mama cat supervised her orange tom and gray female as they clambered and pounced on hay bales, while Bruno checked out the loft.

"You don't think they'll run away?" Cody still couldn't muster up the courage to discuss their past, so he kept coming up with inane subject matter.

"You fed them." She scratched the mama calico along her cheek. "So they should stay close here."

Cody settled on a hay bale. Would his leg ever stop aching?

A breeze wafted through the barn, stirring strands that had strayed from her braid around her face. Absolutely beautiful. Why hadn't some man snapped her up? Was it because of all the homeless pets she kept? Cody loved animals as much as she did, but not everyone felt the same way.

If she'd found some critter-loving man and were living happily ever after, would it make whatever was left of his life easier or harder? "How come you never married?"

"Excuse me?" She propped her hands on her hips.

"Just curious." He shrugged. "Back when we were in high school, you dreamed right along with Caitlyn about getting married."

"I did, didn't I?" Her voice went soft and she settled on a hay bale facing him, elbows propped on her knees. "My parents married right out of high school and Mom never worked outside the home. She didn't have a clue about how to get a job, balance the checkbook or pay the bills."

She picked up the gray kitten and cuddled it. "Dad had done everything for her. For a while after he died, I thought I'd have to give up college and stay home to take care of her. It made me realize I never want to need anyone that much."

"Everybody needs somebody."

"Look who's talking." She caught his gaze. "Mr. I'm-Never-Getting-Married-so-I-Can-Travel-and-Do-What-I-Want."

"I guess it got old." But it really hadn't. Not until he'd seen her again. Only one thing was certain. Being close to her drove it home. If he didn't have a bubble in his head, he'd go after way more than friendship with Ally.

He had to stop thinking about things he couldn't pursue. "I could build you a few extra pens above the ones you already have to solve your cat problem."

"I'd always planned to do that, just haven't had time." She bit her lip. "That would be great, but if you really want to help me, there is something else you can do."

"Just ask."

"Would you sell me a few acres? I had my eye on five, but one would get me out of a bind."

He'd have loved to. But the problem with that was that he was only leasing. Yet he needed his family to believe he was willingly retiring to become a rancher. Otherwise, they'd get curious and if they learned about his health situation, they'd hover and he'd have no peace while he decided what to do.

He couldn't burden her with his secret.

"Well?"

"Ally?" A man's voice called out, cutting off any response he might have given her.

"Over in the neighbor's barn," she yelled.

Footfalls crunched across the gravel and a shadow fell over the doorway.

A gray-haired man wearing scrubs stepped inside. "Everything go okay with the mastiff?"

"She'll be fine." She nodded. "The car just grazed her. Lacerations and contusions, but no internal injuries or broken bones. Most of her damage came from the highway."

"Ouch." The man winced. "Poor girl. I finished the vaccinations. Derek filled out all the records and he's putting the ranch file in the office. Just thought I'd check in before I go."

Ally gestured to the man. "This is Dr. Lance Bridges, the other vet here at my clinic. Cody is our new neighbor. He took Bruno and the three strays I got in yesterday, just in the knick of time. I'll tell you all about it tomorrow."

"Nice meeting you." Cody clasped hands with Lance.

"Likewise."

"You go on home. I'm sure Erin has your supper ready."

"See you tomorrow." As Dr. Bridges turned away, a younger man approached. Blond, midtwenties.

"Some first day, huh, Derek?"

"I loved every minute of it." The younger man smiled, scratched the kitten Ally held under its chin. His hand dangerously close to hers.

Huh? Was he flirting with Ally?

Was this guy an assistant? Or working on being her boyfriend?

Ally pushed stray strands of hair away from her face. "You tell that sweet wife of yours I'll try not to keep you this late on a daily basis."

Whew. Thankfully the guy was married.

But what should it matter? Ally's love life was none of Cody's concern. It couldn't be.

"Don't worry. Brandy understands my work." The guy turned to the door.

"Where are my manners?" Ally stood, brushed the hay off the seat of her jeans. "This is Cody Warren. We were friends all through school, and now he lives next door. Derek Tatum is my new veterinary technician."

"It's nice to meet you. I'll see you tomorrow, Ally."

"Make that Tuesday. Have a nice, long Labor Day weekend. With so many ranches in Aubrey, we have more cattle vacs scheduled as usual. But maybe there won't be any emergencies."

"But you're working tomorrow and Monday. If it's all the same to you, I'd just as soon do the same."

"If you're sure."

"I am." With a wave, Derek left them alone.

Ally set the kitten down and it curled around her ankle. "So what about the land?"

He'd hoped she'd forget about the issue. "I can't sell you any of it."

"Why not?" Her shoulders slumped. "Just an acre? A half an acre?"

His only option was to be as honest as he could. "I'm only leasing it." What were the odds of her talking to his parents about his land anyway?

"But yesterday you said you bought it."

"No, you said I bought it. I decided to test the ranching thing out before doing anything permanent." Great. He'd just reinforced her notion that he had commitment issues.

"Oh." The corners of her mouth tipped down and she stood. "I'm really tired and I can't wait to get cleaned up. Do you want me to walk you across the yard?"

It was tempting to lean on her. But not advisable.

"I'll be fine. I'll go nice and slow." He opened the door for her.

She exited and he followed. By the time he'd made five steps, she'd already reached her back door. Not sparing him another glance, she slipped inside and closed it.

So much for talking about the kiss. It seemed as if without saying a word, they both agreed to forget it. At least things weren't quite as strained between them. Though maybe that would've been preferable.

Ally was his friend. And that was all she could be. So why did he have to keep reminding himself of that?

Ally stepped into the mudroom, where excited yips greeted her. "Hey, Foxy. Hey, Wolf." The two puffballs danced for her attention. "Did y'all miss me today?"

Peering through the blinds, she watched Cody slowly hobble to his house. He'd saved her from a written reprimand. But he wouldn't sell her any land, because he was only leasing. Which meant he probably wasn't staying.

He frustrated the daylights out of her. So she wouldn't coddle him. He was an adult. If he was goofy enough to insist on living alone and walking on his bad leg without any help, that was his problem. She didn't have the time or energy to babysit him while he played rancher next door. On the land he'd leased right out from under her.

She pulled off her manure-caked boots and picked a Pom up in each arm, snuggling them close. They stilled, except for their noses.

"Busted. Mama traitored—petting countless other dogs and cats again." The sniffing stopped and kisses took over. With both cheeks sufficiently licked, she set them down.

"Mom?"

"In the living room. Did the emergency surgery go okay?"

"Yep, she'll be fine. Derek was a great help to Lance with the vaccinations." She strolled into the living room. Home. She loved this house. The worn plank flooring and walls, beams across the ceilings, and ancient windows. Comfortable, unpretentious and cozy.

"Did Dr. Bridges leave already?" Mom was in her jammies, curled up on the couch with a book.

"A few minutes ago." Ally couldn't wait to soak in the bathtub for an hour. Except for Mom's weekly book club meetings, they both were usually in for the evening by six o'clock. Such exciting lives they led. Probably should get out more.

Maybe she'd have more oomph at the end of the day with Derek around. Most applicants would have waited until Tuesday to start work, but she was thankful for his eagerness.

Today's ranch vaccinations had been so much easier with help, and when she'd gotten the emergency call, Derek had been able to stay with Lance and finish. Best of all, she didn't ache quite as much with an extra set of hands at work.

Wolf and Foxy pranced circles around her, offering un-

conditional love—even though she'd been with other critters all day.

"Y'all don't care who I play with, do ya?" Her high-
pitched tone sent the tiny bundles of energy into excited
jitters and she settled on the floor, leaning against the
couch. The Poms fought for lap space, then stilled as she
stroked their soft coats. "You'll never guess who showed
up after you left, though."

"I saw you with Cody after I got out of the shower."

"He arrived just as the state inspector was about to write
me up for having too many cats. Cody took Bruno and the
three I got in yesterday and saved the day." And rubbed
her shoulders. She could still feel his touch.

"I wonder why the inspector came again. Good thing
Cody was there to be your hero."

"Until I asked him to sell me an acre and he admitted
he's only leasing the land." She picked up Foxy and rubbed
noses with her. "What's up with that, Foxy?"

The only problem with furry friends—they never answered back.

Wolf let out a yip.

Not in people language, anyway.

"Maybe once his lease is up, you can buy the acreage.
It'll work out." Mom gave her an encouraging smile. "Just
have faith."

Mom's words stung. Faith was exactly what she didn't
have.

Why couldn't her new neighbor have been someone
else? A single woman living alone, or a family with a mom
who needed adult companionship. Someone who could
have at least sold her an acre or two. And who didn't stir
such confusing feelings in her. Even some animal-hating
grouch. Anyone other than landlocking Cody.

Though he probably wouldn't even stay put. Which, as

her mom had pointed out, could be good for her. He wouldn't even be here if not for his injuries and she was sure he'd head back to the circuit just as soon as he could hobble there.

If Cody moved on, she'd get another chance to convince the owner to sell her a parcel of the land. But that meant Cody would run out on her like before. When she'd needed him most. She had to stay away from him in order to survive this go-round.

For as long as she could remember, Cody had gone from one obsession to the next, never sticking with anything for long. Baseball, basketball, fishing, hunting, soccer, football, racquetball and finally rodeo. He'd pursued rodeo far longer than anything else.

Wolf was hanging off her lap and Ally shifted her legs into a crisscross position to give the dogs more room. Closing her eyes, she twirled the end of her braid around her finger.

Sometimes she could still imagine it was her dad doing it. Even after twelve years, she longed for his presence, his sound counsel. He'd have known what to do about her shelter. But he wasn't here.

"Ally?"

She looked up. Mom had clearly asked her something. "What?"

"Are you ready for supper?"

"You can go ahead. I need a bath."

Her only hope was to buy the land once Cody got bored with playing rancher and his lease was done. And that would be best for her wayward heart, too.

A hot bath and a bowl of soup later, she crawled in bed thinking about her predicament.

And Cody. She wouldn't be his new short-term diversion.

Stop thinking about him.

She closed her eyes and snuggled under the covers—exhaustion fogging her brain.

Dogs barking. Ally opened her eyes. Lots of yapping. And they were close. How long had she slept—minutes or hours? It was still dark outside. She was used to the sound. In fact, she usually woke up only when they weren't barking. But this frenzied chorus seemed to come from right under her window.

She rolled over, squinted at the green digital numbers on her clock. Four twenty-three. Why were the dogs stirred up in the wee hours of the morning? And why did they sound so near? She threw the covers back, jumped up and hurried to the window.

Three dogs surrounded the live oak in her yard. Barks, yips and growls filled the early-morning air. As her eyes adjusted to the moonlight, she spotted a cat clinging to a gnarled, twisted limb high in the tree. In the distance, the lights were on in the barn.

What were they doing loose? Her heart lodged in her throat. She flipped her lamp on, tugged a warm-up suit over her pajamas and darted down the hall.

"Mom." Ally knocked on her bedroom door. "The animals are loose." Flashlight in hand, she bolted through the house and jerked the front door open. A light blinded her as she barreled into something solid.

Someone solid.

She screamed.

Chapter Three

"It's me." Cody's strong arms steadied her. The soft flannel of his shirt warmed her against the chill of the night air as his familiar spicy scent surrounded her.

Ally pulled away from him. "Are you all right? I didn't hurt your knee, did I?"

"No." He lowered the beam of his flashlight and she got a glimpse of his denim clad legs. "Why are the animals out?"

"I have no idea."

"I'll help you corral them."

"You can't." She stepped around him. "It's dark and you'll step in a hole or something and hurt your knee. If you want to help, though, go to the barn. I'll catch the dogs and bring them to you. Just put them in pens and I'll sort out who goes where later. Once I get all the dogs, then I'll be able to lure the cats back."

"I'm on it." He limped toward the barn.

She ran to the clinic. The door stood wide open. Odd. She grabbed several collars with leashes and a handful of treats, then scurried back out to the gathering under the tree.

"Here, Spot." The splotched mutt ignored her as he jumped, his front paws running up the tree with each lunge as he growled at the terrified cat. "I've got treats." She dug a biscuit out of her pocket and held it just out of the dog's reach. Spot's nose twitched and he lost interest in the cat long enough for her to clasp a collar around his neck. "Gotcha."

She stood on his leash while she went through the same routine with the Border collie mix and the terrier mix. With all three dogs leashed, she tugged them with all her might toward the barn.

A flashlight beam shone from the house. "What can I do?" Mom hollered.

"Catch dogs. Then we'll worry about the cats."

"I called Lance—I mean Dr. Bridges—to help."

A truck turned into her drive. Lance? No, he couldn't have gotten here from Denton so quickly. Who could it be? *Please not an emergency.* Pressure mounted in her chest.

The engine died and doors slammed. "Hey, it's Raquel. Cody called us to help."

Ally could have cheered. "Y'all are awesome." The Walkers were her closest neighbors other than Cody. Ally usually handled the health needs of their four-legged menagerie.

"How many are accounted for?" Slade, Raquel's husband, hurried to take the three unruly dogs from Ally.

"I'm not even sure." Ally scanned the area with her flashlight. "These are the only ones I've caught. I didn't want Cody hobbling around in the dark, so he's in the barn waiting to put them away as I catch them."

"Hunter, you help Mom catch dogs." Slade roughed up the young boy's already tousled hair with his free hand. Although the dogs fought against the leashes, he didn't budge. "I'll haul this rowdy handful to Cody and then Ally can see who's missing. I'll be right back to help."

"I'm so grateful y'all came." Ally surveyed the threesome clad in wrinkled jeans and jackets.

"This is gonna be fun." Seven-year-old Hunter darted around the back of the house.

"Watch for snakes," Raquel called.

"Probably too cool for them and I don't usually have any in the yard." Ally jogged to the barn, opened the door for Slade and took a quick inventory.

Some of the missing were boarders. She had to find them and keep this incident quiet. Strays roaming free could jeopardize her shelter. But if word got out that people's pets had gotten loose, her clients would lose trust in her.

As she stepped outside, another truck pulled in the drive. The door opened and shut. "How many are loose?" Lance's flashlight bobbed his approach.

"Thirteen dogs, nineteen cats—some strays and some boarders. Not all of them at least. I'm sorry to drag you out this time of night all the way from Denton."

"It's only fifteen minutes and we're in this together."

Over the next couple of hours, Hunter caught two dogs, while Slade rounded up three. Raquel manhandled a smaller breed and Lance nabbed another, while Ally wrangled an elusive wienie dog boarder who seemed intent on playing hide-and-seek.

"I heard some barking in the woods behind the barn." Slade headed back out. "Raquel, Hunter, y'all stay here— might be dangerous."

"Be careful." Raquel shuddered.

"I'll go with you." Lance followed.

Hunter and Raquel helped soothe the dogs, and as the sun began to rise, Slade and Lance returned with the last two Lab mixes.

"What about the cats?" Hunter helped her get the last two in their pens.

"They won't come out unless it's quiet and calm." Ally

hugged Raquel. "Thanks so much for coming. I'd still be at it if y'all hadn't."

"We were glad to help. Hunter had a blast." Raquel tousled his hair. "You can tell all your friends about your dog-wrangling skills."

"Um…about that." Ally bit her lip. "Would y'all mind keeping this incident quiet? I don't want the people who board their pets here to lose confidence in my services."

"Good point." Slade gripped Hunter's shoulder. "Hear that? We're keeping this a secret." Hunter nodded and Slade turned to his wife. "We better go so Ally can tend to her cats."

The threesome waved goodbye as Ally thanked them again.

"Go home, Lance. Get some rest. I can handle things here today."

"Not happening. Saturday's always our busiest. If your mom will ply me with coffee, I'll be good to go."

"Great idea." Mom covered her yawn and the two strolled toward the house.

Leaving only Cody. "You should get some sleep. All I have to do is call the cats."

"I'll stick around." He scanned the pens lining each side of the long barn. "I doubt any of the dogs are in the pens they're supposed to be in. Once you retrieve the cats, I'll help you sort it out. Besides, I need to talk to you."

"Okay." *About what?* "Can it wait?"

"Go call your cats. It'll keep."

"I'll be back as quick as I can." She dug a stack of collapsed cardboard carriers from the storage closet, tucked them under her arm. "And thanks for all your help."

"My pleasure."

Ally stepped out. Cody seemed so serious. Had he talked to the owner? Would he sell her the land after all?

* * *

"Here, kitty, kitty, kitty." Ally's call was a gentle singsong as Cody watched from the barn window.

It took several minutes, but the cats started coming. From trees, from the roof, from the loft and from the woods. Soon she had them in cardboard kennels, and she pulled her truck near to load them.

Cody couldn't stand watching her do all the work. It had nearly killed him to let Slade and Lance play dogcatcher while he stayed in the barn. It was daylight now—easier to watch for holes. He limped out to help.

"What are you doing out here?"

"At least let me load them for you, save you a little work." He made his way to the truck bed.

"Fine." She picked up a kennel. "Stack them in twos and make sure they're stable. I don't want them tumbling around and scarring their delicate sensibilities for life."

"Cats have sensibilities?" He grinned.

"They most certainly do. Very delicate ones."

"I guess if anybody knows about it, it would be you." Cody loaded a kennel she handed him. "You looked like the Pied Piper out there gathering them all up."

"Just call me the crazy cat lady."

"You must be exhausted."

"You, too." She adjusted a stack of kennels. "I can't believe the Walkers came over to help so early. How do you even know them?"

"Raquel's first husband was a Texas Ranger and Mitch's partner. A few years after he died, Mitch tried to fix us up, but neither of us was interested and she eventually met Slade."

He slid another kennel in place. "Slade used to be a chaplain on the rodeo circuit, so I'd seen him around. They're good folk. Since Raquel's the school nurse and it's Saturday, and Slade's a preacher and it isn't Sunday, I knew they could come without messing up the rest of their day."

"I couldn't even think of any of that. I was in panic mode."

"Speaking of panic, I don't mean to scare you—" A cat yowled at him as he hoisted its kennel on top of another "—but you don't have any enemies, do you?"

"Not that I know of." She stopped, caught his gaze. "Why?"

"That's what I wanted to talk to you about." Cody's heart thudded. He really didn't want to frighten her, but she seemed so oblivious. "Somebody had to have let them out."

"But why would they?" She hugged herself. "I must have left a couple of the pens open."

"Have you ever done that before?"

"No. But I've been distracted."

True. The almost reprimand from the inspector. The land Cody couldn't sell her. "Even if you left a couple of pens open, that doesn't explain how thirteen dogs and nineteen cats got out. You don't really think one of each got out, then nosed all the other locks until they opened like it happens in the movies?"

"Of course not." She huffed out a sigh, shoved another pet carrier at him. "But I don't know why anyone would let them out."

"Maybe somebody wants to shut you down." He settled the last cat in place, striving for casual, trying not to let her see how worried he was. "Think about it—you said your state inspector must have gotten a complaint to show up when he did, and now your critters are loose in the middle of the night."

"But no one lives anywhere near here." She spread her hands wide, gesturing to miles of endless woods and pastures surrounding their properties. "Just you and me. Who would want to shut me down?"

"What about Lance?"

"No. I've known him a couple of years. He's a nice man, a member of our church."

"Maybe he wants to buy you out?"

"He had his own clinic in Denton and sold it to work toward retirement."

"What do you really know about Derek?"

"He's a great guy. I can't tell you how much it helped to have another set of hands on duty yesterday."

"You're sure he's okay?"

"Positive." She shook her head. "He has no reason to want to shut me down."

"Maybe he wants his own practice."

"No. He's a tech. The only way he can do anything is under the supervision of a licensed vet."

But Cody wasn't so sure. Maybe he needed his Texas Ranger brother to do a background check on Derek. And Lance. Ally's safety was too important to risk.

She was way too important to him. Way more important than he should allow her to be.

It felt good to attend the church Cody had grown up in. How many years had it been since he'd been here? When he'd visited home for the holidays while on the circuit, he'd often gone with his sister in Dallas, with his brother when he'd lived in Garland or with Grandpa in Medina. Over the years, he'd only attended his home church a handful of times.

As morning class dismissed, he caught up with Mitch. "Can we talk a minute?"

"Sure."

Metal chairs scraped the tiled floor and multiple conversations started up.

Cody waited until the classroom emptied. "Can you run a background check on Derek Tatum for me?"

"Why?"

"I think somebody's trying to shut Ally's shelter down."

"What gives you that idea?"

"This has to stay quiet." She'd tan his hide if she knew what he was up to. "Ally's worried it'll hurt her shelter's reputation."

"My lips are sealed."

"Someone turned several of her animals loose the other night," Cody whispered, even though they were alone.

"You're sure it wasn't a faulty latch?"

"Thirty or so faulty latches? How about Lance Bridges—know anything about him?"

"Isn't he the other vet at her clinic?"

"Can you run a check on him, too?"

"I need probable cause, little brother." Mitch folded his arms across his chest—his stubborn stance. "I can't just run a check on random citizens because you want me to."

"How much probable cause did you have when you ran a check on each of your wife's employees?"

"What makes you think I did that?"

"I know you."

Mitch's Adam's apple bobbed. "Touché."

Cody sighed. "I'm worried about Ally's safety."

"I'll see what I can find."

"Thanks."

The brothers exited the classroom, strolled into the sanctuary and claimed their seats on each side of Mitch's wife Caitlyn. Old-fashioned pews lined the church with traditional hymnals in the book racks, and prisms of multicolored light radiated through the stained-glass windows.

Even after his years away, it was still home. New preacher, new Sunday-school teacher, new pianist, even a new song leader, but the same timeless hymns. He still knew most of the congregation, and a lot of the new faces he'd seen on the circuit over the years. But the most important member—to him—was nowhere in sight.

"Where's Ally?" Cody elbowed Caitlyn, trying for casual.

"She doesn't come anymore." Caitlyn grabbed a hymnal from the book rack. "Not since her dad died."

"Really?" Why would Ally turn away from God after her dad died? That was when she'd needed Him most.

"You two are neighbors now. Haven't you seen her?"

"Well, yeah. But we didn't talk about church."

The pianist played louder as a deacon approached the pulpit to begin announcements. "Welcome. We hope you enjoy our services today. All of the announcements are in your bulletin, but we have one pressing need. Our volunteer couple who'd signed up to supply animals and oversee the petting zoo at our annual church carnival had a family emergency out of town." He checked his notes.

"Looks like they had most of the plans for the petting zoo in place, but with the carnival this weekend, we'll need volunteers ASAP. We have several gentle horses, but we still need a few more small animals and two volunteers to oversee both. If interested, see our director after services." The deacon turned the service over to the song director.

Ally could provide dogs and cats, and she'd probably know where to find more animals. Maybe he could talk her into volunteering to supply the petting zoo and help him oversee it. It would help the church, she might find homes for some of her strays, and it could get her back in church.

But how should he go about convincing her to agree?

* * *

At least the week started off quiet. Routine appointments. No emergencies. No state inspectors. No loose animals.

A tiny golden Chihuahua mix shivered in the corner of her crate. From nerves, not temperature. Ally fished her out.

"Poor baby Buttercup." Ally snuggled the tiny shaking body against her chest. "My poor little runt. Your brother and sister found families, but don't give up. You'll get your forever home. I promise."

"There you are." Cody's voice echoed through the long barn.

Ally's heart sped as yips, barks and howls started up. She stepped out of the pen into the alley between the kennels.

"What are you doing here?"

"I could ask you the same thing." Cody limped toward her, leaning on his cane. "It's Labor Day. Don't you believe in taking a day off?"

"Staying open was convenient for my clients who were off work today."

"Well, since you like staying busy—" he stopped beside her, too close "—I have a proposal for you."

Her breathing sputtered. Not that kind of proposal. And she wouldn't fall for it if it was.

"Who's this little guy?" Cody scratched the quivering puppy between her ears.

"She. Her name is Buttercup. She and two littermates were found in the baseball park this past spring. Her brother and sister were adopted, but she's the runt. No one has picked her yet."

"My sister, Tara, loves Chihuahuas and hers died a few months ago." He lifted the puppy out of her arms and tenderly held the quivering body against his heart. "Maybe she'll take this little darling."

"She's not all Chihuahua and that's probably why she got dumped."

"Tara's not a breed snob. Who could dump a sweetie like this?" Cody baby-talked the puppy as she buried her nose in his neck.

"I don't have a clue." Ally's frustration came out in her tone. "At least there was a ball game that night. One of the moms found them and brought them to me."

"So which of these dogs and cats are homeless?" The chorus of barks had settled as the dogs got used to him in their midst.

"I keep the first twenty kennels on the left for boarding. Their people are gone on vacation or out of town for work reasons."

"Their people?" Cody grinned.

"I don't call them owners. We think of animals as our pets, so I figure the pets think of us as their people."

"Why is she shaking? It's not cold in here."

"Chihuahuas have an abundance of energy. She needs a walk. I was just about to take her for one." The Border collie–spaniel mix stuck his white-and-black muzzle through his fence and whimpered. "I know, baby. You want some attention, too." She rubbed his snout.

"Can I take him for a walk?"

"Probably not a good idea with your leg. But you can sit with him if you want."

"I'd love that. In fact, point out the ones who need some attention and I'll take care of it while you're gone."

He certainly wasn't making her heart grow any less fond of him by being so sweet and concerned over her strays. "You sure?"

"It's not like I have anything else to do."

"Okay, hit this side." She gestured to the pens on the right. "Love on as many as you can or want to."

"Will do." He headed for the first pen, then snapped his fingers and turned back toward her. "I almost forgot my proposal. I went to our old church yesterday and signed you up to supply the pets and oversee the petting zoo for the carnival this weekend."

Her neck heated. Was that steam blowing out her ears? "Without asking me?"

"It was a spur-of-the-moment thing and they needed volunteers fast or the whole thing was threatening to fall apart." He shrugged. "They'd already advertised the petting zoo, so they have to supply it. And just think, it might be a chance to get some of your strays adopted out."

"But I don't go to church there anymore." She propped her hands on her hips.

"I know. Caitlyn told me."

"So did you ever stop to think maybe I'm tied up with my church this weekend? Or with work? Or with life?" Not that she had one, really, but he didn't need to know that.

"Your church? You still go?"

"Of course I go." She was a glorified pew warmer, just going through the motions, but she wouldn't mention that. "There are other churches, you know."

"I just assumed. Caitlyn said you hadn't been since…"

Her dad died. Her eyes stung. "I haven't. Mom and I switched to one in Denton."

"Did something happen at our church?"

"No." She sat down on a hay bale. "It was just overwhelming. Everybody was so sympathetic and sad for us. The sympathy almost smothered us. We wanted to go somewhere where nobody knew us. Where nobody knew Dad." Her voice wobbled. "Where they didn't feel sorry for us." Where Ally could pretend she was still leaning on God.

The hay bale gave with his weight as he sat beside her. "They were sad for you because they care."

"I know." She swiped at her eyes. "It was just too much."

He put an arm around her shoulders.

Ally's pulse thrummed at his nearness. In fact, he could probably hear it. More than anything, she wanted to snuggle close, accept his comfort.

For a breath of a second, she let her head rest against his shoulder. But if she stayed, she might lose her heart. And he'd realize how she felt. But she couldn't feel that way about him or any other man. Self-sufficient Ally didn't need anyone. Wouldn't allow herself to. She pulled away from him and stood.

"I'll make a few calls, see if I can rustle up animals for the petting zoo."

"And think about overseeing it? It starts after school lets out Friday and ends at seven. Then ten till three on Saturday."

"Sorry, those are my work hours." She scooped the puppy away from Cody, touching him as little as possible. "I need to walk Buttercup. You start dog-sitting while I go." She grabbed a leash off the wall and strode toward the exit.

"Hey, Ally."

"Hmm." She stopped but didn't turn around.

"Are you mad at me?"

Yes. I'm mad at you for leasing my land. For that stupid kiss and leaving me behind all those years ago. But she couldn't tell him that. And that wasn't what he meant anyway.

Her shoulders slumped. "No. But in the future, don't sign me up for anything without asking me first."

"I meant about the kiss."

Chapter Four

Great. Cody held his breath. Maybe she'd think that break in his voice came from the awkward subject.

"What kiss?" Ally kept her back to him.

She didn't remember? Had it meant so little to her? Could the same kiss that turned Cody's world upside down be forgettable for her? Oh, how he wished he hadn't brought it up. Especially since his emotions had betrayed him. But he had and he couldn't let it drop.

"After your dad— I got carried away with comforting you. I was a kid and you were so close to me. You smelled good and I just wanted to make you feel better." You smelled good? Just shut up, Warren. Before you say something else stupid and make it even worse.

"It didn't mean anything." Her response was little more than a whisper.

"I know." To her, anyway. His heart crashed on the concrete between his boots. "I just want you to know—you're safe from me. So if you ever need a shoulder, I'm not a kid anymore. I can do just comfort."

"Good to know." She latched the leash on Buttercup's collar and vaulted out of the barn.

Cody stood and looked skyward. "You're safe from

me?" he muttered and ran a hand through his hair. It sounded dumb, and with everything in him, he wanted to take it back.

But at least maybe things would be easier between them now. He'd help her with her animals and, if she agreed, the carnival so her strays might be adopted. And deep down, so he could spend time with her.

On top of everything else, he'd lied to her. He hadn't signed her up for the petting zoo. But telling her he had was the only way he could think of to convince her to participate. *But, Lord, it's for Your good. It'll help the church. And maybe some of Ally's strays will find a home. So yes, I lied and I'm doing it for the wrong reasons, but You can take my selfish intentions and work them for good.*

The Border collie whimpered.

"Hey, guy. What's your name?" Cody read the plate by the gate. "Oreo." He unlatched the pen and stepped inside. In the corner, he sat on a chair and the dog reared up on his knees. "A fitting name."

Ally was the kind of woman who named each stray. The kind of woman he could spend the rest of his life with. But how much life did he have left?

He had to be satisfied with being her friend. Only her friend.

Oreo settled his chin on Cody's knee. "You wanna come home with me, don't you, boy?" The dog's ears perked up. "I think I'll tell Ally to hold you for me until I get a bit more steady on my feet."

His phone rang and he dug it out of his pocket. Mitch. "Hello?"

"Those persons of interest we discussed. No record. Upstanding citizens."

"You're sure?"

"We're talking Boy Scouts. Literally. Any more trouble?"

"No." Cody scratched between the dog's ears. "Maybe I'm barking up the wrong tree—pun intended."

"I hope so. You let me know if there are any more incidents."

"I will. Thanks." Cody ended the call.

Maybe the other night had been an accident. Kids playing a prank or taking a dare. Doubtful, but maybe. Or maybe it was just a onetime thing. Just in case, he had to stick close to Ally. To make sure she stayed safe.

But how could he keep his heart in check while he protected her?

Her mom and the volunteers from the youth group traipsed the property with various dogs while Ally walked the Border collie spaniel.

The kiss discussion was a whole day ago, but her heartbeat hadn't gotten back to normal yet.

She smelled good. Cody thought she smelled good. Back in high school, anyway.

Now she smelled like…horse sweat, manure and worse.

But twelve years ago, had Cody been attracted to her?

No, she'd just been sad and he'd wanted to make her feel better. She knew it then and she knew it now. Why couldn't her heart catch on?

If he'd felt anything for her, he wouldn't have left for the rodeo, wouldn't have stayed gone so long.

And besides, she did not need a man in her life. Not Cody. Or anyone else. She had to stop thinking about him and concentrate on finding homes for her strays.

Gravel crunched in her drive.

Past her regular hours, clients with emergencies tended to make frantic calls first, and her usual volunteers had already arrived and were walking dogs.

"Let's go see who it is, Oreo." She turned the dog back toward the clinic.

As she rounded the building Cody headed toward the barn.

With a woman.

Her heart stammered. His girlfriend? Fiancée?

She couldn't do this. Meet the woman in Cody's life. Not with her hair more out of her braid than in. Not with manure on her boots. She turned away and tried to hurry Oreo out of their sight.

"Ally, there you are," Cody called.

Ally's shoulders fell. Out of all the horse ranches in Aubrey, why had the one next to her stayed vacant until Cody Warren decided to play ranch?

"Ally, over here."

Straightening her shoulders, she pasted a smile on her face and turned around.

"Hey." Feet forward, one step at a time.

Way too fast, the gap between them closed. The woman looked familiar.

"This is my dog." Cody bent to scratch Oreo. "Or he will be when I get a bit more recovered."

For you or for your girlfriend?

"We bonded last night, didn't we, boy? I'd take him now if it wasn't for my knee, but Ally's holding him for me." Cody looked up at her. "You remember my sister, Tara?"

His sister. Ally looked past the blond hair, recognized the familiar green eyes and smile. "Of course." A fit of relieved laughter clogged in her throat. Did she sound as giddy as she felt?

"It's great to see you." Tara hugged her.

"You, too. I didn't recognize you at first."

"Well, what can I say?" Tara patted her locks. "I'm a hairdresser. When I get bored, I change my color. So, where is she?" Tara rubbed her hands together much the same way Cody did when anticipating food.

"She who?"

"Remember?" Cody winked at her. "I told you to hold Buttercup until I could check with Tara?"

The wink rattled her already-shaky heart. "Oh. Of course. You'd like to see her."

"Actually, I want to take her home."

"Without meeting her first? She's not full-blood."

"I know and I was reluctant at first, but not because of her breeding." Tara's eyes misted and she pressed a hand to her chest. "I've still got footprints on my heart from Ginger and I initially said no. But Cody told me how sweet Buttercup is and showed me a picture. I couldn't resist, so here I am."

"That's wonderful." Ally transferred Oreo's leash from one hand to the other as the dog grew restless. "I know you'll provide a good home for her. But there are a few things to consider before you see her. Didn't you get married?"

"Yes. We live in Dallas."

"Does your husband like dogs?"

"Oh, yes. Jared is a major animal lover." Tara's smile turned dreamy. "I wouldn't have married him if he wasn't."

"What about children?"

"Not yet, but definitely planned in the future."

"Chihuahuas aren't the best breed with small children." Oreo persisted in wrapping his leash around Ally's legs. "They can be protective of their people and aggressive, so they've been known to nip toddlers for simply climbing into Mommy's lap."

"I didn't realize." Tara's eyes widened.

"But she's not all Chihuahua. So it may not be an issue and if it is, if properly trained or kept separate until the child is older, there shouldn't be a problem."

"Oh, good."

"Now, what about where you live?" Ally stepped out of the corkscrew Oreo had created. "Apartment? House? Do you have a yard?"

"We're in a subdivision, a house with a fenced-in yard." Tara knelt to scratch behind Oreo's ears. "We kept Ginger in the mudroom with a doggy door while we were gone. Whoever got home first romped with her in the backyard and sometimes we'd take her for a walk in the evening. When we were home, she had the run of the house."

Ally offered her hand. "You pass. Buttercup is yours if you want her."

"I do. Let's go get her." Tara stood and rubbed her hands together again.

"Let me walk him back." Cody took Oreo's leash, his hand grazing Ally's. Electricity shot all the way to her toes.

While it took food to excite Cody, and Buttercup got Tara animated, it seemed Cody was Ally's source of excitement. His nearness propelled her right over the edge of her sanity.

Which was why she'd held off on agreeing to volunteer for the carnival. Spending a day and a half with him certainly wouldn't help her keep her right mind. But time at the church with her other two dozen or so four-legged friends who still needed forever homes would be good advertisement.

More than anything, she wanted to help the abandoned pets in her care. But could she survive working side by side with Cody?

It had taken Tara forever to finalize her purchases—a crate, a leash, a chew toy, along with tick-and-flea preventative—before she'd taken Buttercup and been on her way.

Cody loved his sister, but he was dying to spend time with Ally alone.

"So, you're holding Oreo for me, right?"

"I told you I would." Ally pointed to the boarding side of the kennels. "See, I moved him over to the boarder side last night. He belongs to someone."

"Do I need to pay you for boarding him?"

"No. He's fine until you can take him home."

"I wish I could right now." Cody sat on a hay bale and scratched the dog's head. "Let me at least provide his food."

"I'm just glad he has a home. Whenever you're well enough, he's yours."

"You hear that, buddy?" The pup's ears perked up at the enthusiasm in Cody's voice. He already loved the dog.

"And now that you're in the longhorn business, Oreo is great with cattle."

"So you know his history?"

"His former owner brought him here because Oreo insisted on herding her horses."

"His former owner? Not his person?"

"She obviously was never Oreo's person." Ally harrumphed. "I guess I should be glad she brought him here instead of dumping him. Thanks for finding Buttercup a home."

"I thought you weren't going to let Tara have her for a minute there."

"I was just being cautious." Ally raked hay out of a kennel and replaced it with a fresh batch. "I know Tara would never dump a dog, but a lot of the reason there are so many strays is because people aren't prepared to have a pet. Some breeds have more issues than others, so I make sure my potential adoptive families understand what they're getting into."

"I'm glad she passed. She'd already fallen in love with Buttercup."

"Actually, Tara got the brief version since she's owned a Chihuahua before. If she hadn't, I'd have gone into the chewing-on-the-couch issues." The barking around them reached a crescendo as the last of the volunteers exited. "If the potential adoptive family has thought through all aspects of having a pet, there's more of a chance that both the pet and their person will be happy."

"So why didn't you grill me about Oreo before you agreed to let me be his person?"

"Because I know you. I remember how much you loved Duke. How patient you were with him. Even as a kid. And I know you'll love Oreo and take care of him."

Memories of his first dog warmed Cody's insides. That Ally remembered did funny things in his chest.

"You'll take care of him no matter where you end up."

No matter where he ended up? Apparently he hadn't convinced her he was settling in Aubrey yet. Even though his longhorns arrived yesterday and she was vaccinating them tomorrow. Maybe he should've had a little faith and bought the ranch instead of leasing it.

The phone rang and she hurried past the kennels to the desk. "*Ally's Vet Clinic and Adopt-a-Pet.* May I help you?"

Cody scratched Oreo's ears and cooed at him. How did animals reduce full-grown men to baby talk? Probably the same way babies did. Michaela, his niece courtesy of Mitch and Caitlyn, had him making silly faces and doing whatever it took just to get a grin out of her these days.

And made him think about having his own kids someday. If he lived long enough for it.

Ally let out a little whoop, whirled around and came running toward him.

"What?" He stood.

"You're so awesome!" She hugged him.

His arms slid around her waist, sending his pulse into orbit. "I've been trying to convince everyone of that for years."

"That was a friend of Tara's. She said you told her all about my shelter. She's coming tomorrow to get three cats and a dog, maybe even two dogs, for her kids."

"That's wonderful." But not nearly as wonderful as holding her.

She pressed her cheek against his chest, probably hearing his erratic heartbeat. Way too soon, she pushed away from him and their gazes locked. Her face neared his as she rose on tiptoe.

Was she going to kiss him? He closed his eyes in anticipation but her lips brushed his cheek. And then she was gone.

By the time he found enough courage to open his eyes, she was grabbing a leash off the wall.

"My volunteer walkers should get here anytime. You can stay and play with the critters if you want. Oh, and that carnival thing you mentioned. I'll oversee it. I've got ponies, rabbits, goats and, of course, cats and dogs lined up. Is that enough?"

"Sounds great. We still on for tomorrow?"

"Tomorrow? Wednesday? On for what?" She cocked her head to the side.

"You're supposed to vaccinate my cattle."

"Oh. Yes. I'll see you then." She hurried out of the barn.

He pressed his palm against his cheek, trying to capture the sweetness of her lips on his skin as all his dreams puddled on the hay-strewn barn floor.

At least she'd agreed to the carnival. A whole day and a half spent with Ally.

Sorry, God. I know that's not what the carnival is sup-
posed to be about. Help me focus on the kids and not Ally.
It's gonna take lots of work.

Sturdy camouflage muck boots with pink trim and
brown coveralls dwarfed Ally. But somehow she looked
beautiful in the late-afternoon sunlight.

"You sure we'll finish by Bible study time tonight?"
Cody forced his attention to the corral, which teemed with
longhorns, but his gaze bounced right back.

"Piece of cake. This is the last of them." The smudge of
mud that lined her cheekbone didn't take away from her
beauty. But it did give him an excuse to touch her.

He pulled his work glove off and wiped at the smear
with his thumb.

She jerked away. "What?"

"Just some dirt."

She wiped at it with her gloved hand, depositing more
grime.

"You're only making it worse." He chuckled. "And I
think it's more than dirt."

"Eeeeeewwww." Her nose crinkled. "Get it."

Cupping her chin with one hand, he wiped with the
other. And kept wiping long after the suspicious smear
was gone.

Despite their surroundings—a barn lot populated by
fifty longhorns, a dozen ranch hands and two of her employees, all covered in sweat and worse—he still smelled
her fruity shampoo, a hint of vanilla and fresh hay. He
could drown in her milk-chocolate eyes as she looked up
at him with trust.

And there was something else in her gaze. Like she felt
something, too.

She pulled away, pushed stray strands away from her

face with her upper arm and opened the chute. The long-horn they'd just finished with shot forward and one of his ranch hands led the next cow into position with a feed bucket.

They continued that process, and an hour later, Derek gave the final injection, then turned the calf loose. They'd vaccinated all his cattle. Except for stubborn Bessie. The only cow with so much personality he'd already named her. She still stood in the holding pen, refusing to enter the corral to the chute.

"I'll get her." Ally climbed the rail pen.

Halfway up and before she could swing a leg over, Cody caught her foot. "I don't think that's a good idea. Let me send one of my hands in."

"I've done this at least a thousand times." She rolled her eyes and yanked her boot out of his grasp, swung her leg over the rail. "I can handle her."

"You just ran her calf through that chute. Mama cows don't like it when you take their calves."

"Duh." She climbed down inside the pen.

"Be careful." Bessie eyed her warily, the cow's long horns making Cody wary.

"Come on, Bessie." Ally rattled the feed bucket. "Let's get this one little shot done and then you can get on with your day, be back with your baby."

Bessie lowered her head.

"Ally! Get out of there!" Cody clambered up the fence. Heat shot through his knee as his boot slipped.

Bessie pawed the ground.

Ally stood still.

The longhorn charged.

Chapter Five

"Get out, Ally!" Cody's heart stopped.

Derek launched over the rail just to the cow's left and Bessie wheeled toward him as Ally bolted for the opening under the pen. Just before Bessie gored him, Derek climbed the fence, then vaulted over as Bessie rammed her horns into the metal barrier. The steel pin stabilizing the temporary fencing held as Cody jumped down and pulled Ally under to safety.

Bessie spun toward them and charged. Had his ranch hands driven the rest of the steel pins deep enough to hold? *Please, God, keep Ally safe.* He covered her body with his. Would this scare trigger his aneurysm to burst?

Horns rammed against metal and Cody expected hooves on his back. Nothing. He turned to see Bessie staggering in the middle of the pen, shaking her head, slobber trailing from her mouth. He rolled off Ally, stood and helped her up, then dragged her farther away.

Lance pulled off his gloves. "Can one of the hands mount up and drive her?"

"Or a dog." Cody kept his eyes on Ally, making sure she didn't do something stupid again. But from the way she was shaking, she'd probably learned a lesson. "I've got a Border collie."

"Try the dog first. Ally, you go on home, Derek and I will handle her," Lance insisted.

"Be careful." Obviously rattled, she nodded and started for her house.

Cody limped after her, matching his hop-along gait to hers. Once they rounded the barn, out of eyesight, he grabbed her and pulled her into his arms.

She didn't resist, laying her cheek against his shoulder.

"Don't ever do anything like that again."

"I've done it—"

"Thousands of times. But this time almost got you killed." He held her away from him a bit, gave her a gentle shake. "And I couldn't do a thing. I tried to climb in after you. But this stupid bum knee—I slipped and all I could do was watch those horns barreling toward you. All I want is to keep you *safe* and I couldn't."

"I'm fine."

"Just don't do it again." Another scare like that could kill him. "You've got Lance and Derek to handle the difficult ones. Let them. In fact, why don't you stick with dogs and cats and let them deal with the livestock."

"It's part of my job."

"Your critters need you *safe*." He needed her *safe*. "And in one piece. If Oreo does the trick, you're free to take him on every cattle call you get. If not, I'll lend you a ranch hand and a horse. Okay? No more getting in pens with mama cows. Got it?"

"Got it." She searched his face.

Had he given himself away?

He couldn't. Couldn't let her know how he felt when he couldn't promise her a future.

"Now get inside and shower." His hands dropped away

from her shoulders. "You smell like a barn lot." Mixed with the tantalizing smell of Ally. It was so tempting to hold her in his arms again. And never let go. He took a step back, gave her a light shove.

"Do me a favor and don't tell Mom about this." She spun away from him, bolted for her house.

He needed to take lots of steps back. The smartest thing to do would be to move. But the thought of staying away from her completely tore at his insides.

Ally hummed as she strolled toward the barn. It was early morning, barely seventy degrees as the sun warmed her back. Another hour before her clinic opened. Enough time to feed her crew. She turned as movement caught the corner of her eye.

A large dark gray cat with grass-green eyes hunkered near her truck. Oh, no. Were her animals loose again? She scanned the property. Nothing. And come to think of it, she didn't have any cats like this in her shelter right now. Or among her boarders. Probably male, from the size of him.

"Here, kitty, kitty, kitty." She knelt, held her palm up. "I won't hurt you. Here, kitty."

The cat stared her down a moment. Then its stance relaxed.

"Here, kitty, kitty."

The cat trotted in her direction, stopped a few feet away, then slowly inched forward.

"I won't hurt you, sweetie. Do you have a home? Surely no one dumped a pretty kitty like you."

It sniffed her fingers, then rubbed its jaw against her nails and started purring.

"You sure don't act homeless and you look well cared for. In fact, you look familiar. Charcoal?"

The cat looked up at her as if he recognized his name.

"It's you, isn't it?" She picked him up, checked under his tail. Neutered tom. "You are Charcoal. What are you doing all the way out here, boy? Your mama must be worried sick. Let's get you inside and call her."

She headed for the clinic instead of the barn.

"Are they loose again?" Cody stepped off his porch. "I saw you coaxing him."

"No. That's what I thought when I saw him. But I'm pretty sure he belongs to Stetson and Kendra Wright. They're clients and I've taken care of Charcoal since he was a kitten. I'm pretty sure this is him. He must be lost."

"I know them from the rodeo, but they live a good five miles away, clear on the other end of Aubrey."

"I know. It's odd."

"Maybe it's not him." He caught up with her, scratched the cat's chin. Charcoal's purr grew deeper. "All revved up, aren't you, buddy?"

"I was just taking him inside the clinic so I can call Kendra."

"I was fixing to head to the barn to visit the critters."

"Would you mind feeding them? That was my plan, but I need to see to this guy."

"I'm on it." Cody gave the cat one final scratch, his eyes met hers, and he turned away.

If she didn't know better, the way he looked at her... Nonsense. But he'd been really upset yesterday when Bessie had nearly taken her out. He cared and didn't want her to get hurt, because they were friends. Besides, it was his cow terrorizing her, so he'd have felt doubly bad if she'd gotten hurt. That was all.

It had to be all.

She unlocked the clinic door, stepped inside and set the cat down. "You wander where you want while I call your people." She pulled the W drawer, found the file, scanned for the number and dug her cell out of her pocket.

It rang twice and Kendra answered.

"Hey, Kendra, it's Ally. I've got a cat wandering around my place that looks suspiciously like Charcoal."

"How in the world would he get all the way over there? Let me check the barn, see if he's here."

Children's voices chattering in the background. Must be Kendra's young daughter and son. "Mommy's gotta go to the barn. Let's make a train."

Ally's heart took a dip. She didn't want to ever need a man, but that also meant she'd never be a mom. The thought didn't used to bother her. But lately…

"Charcoal," Kendra called. "Here, kitty, kitty, kitty. Charcoal."

The little voices helped call.

"He doesn't seem to be here." Kendra chuckled. "We've roused a barnful of cats, but no Charcoal. And he's usually here ready to eat first thing in the morning."

"I'll put him in a boarding kennel and you can stop by when you get a chance."

"Thanks, Ally. I really appreciate it. I know he prowls at night, but I never imagined him going as far as your place."

It was odd. Ally ended the call, pulled a temporary cardboard kennel from the stack and folded it into shape. "I hate to do this to you, Char. But I'm taking you to the barn and when you hear all those dogs barking, you'll be glad you're in a box." She picked him up and started to set him in the kennel.

He let out a yowl and braced three feet against the card-board.

"It's just for a minute, I promise." She pried his feet loose and closed the lid before he could pop back out, then stuck her finger through one of the large airholes until she felt fur. "It's okay, big guy."

He squalled as she carried him out and toward the barn.

"You're heavy, mister. And you should be quiet. You're letting every dog in the place know you're here."

The yowling continued as she stepped inside the barn and hurried to open a boarding kennel, then opened the box. Charcoal planted himself at the back.

"First you want out, then you want to stay in. Come on, boy." She scooped him up.

By this time, the dogs were in full chorus, and the poor cat was so nervous he willingly dove for the boarding kennel. She fastened the latch in place, then rubbed his cheek through the wire but he didn't purr.

"You'll be okay. I promise. I won't let any of these yappers near you, boy."

"He's the one who started the racket." Cody.

She jumped, spun around.

"Sorry." He sat on a folding chair in Oreo's pen. "I thought you knew I was here."

"No. I called Kendra. She'll pick him up sometime today. Could you feed him while you're at it?"

"Sure. I gave Oreo a little extra after he worked so hard yesterday."

"I can't believe I never thought of using him for vaccinations."

"He's a pro. And I meant what I said—you borrow him for every cattle call. From now on."

From now on. But what about if Cody left? If he went back to the rodeo. Or followed whatever his next diversion turned out to be.

"What if this ranching thing doesn't turn your crank and you leave? What then?"

"If anything happens to me, I want you to have Oreo."

If anything happened to him? Like he might die? Her mouth went dry.

"I mean…if I end up…leaving, I want you to have Oreo for your work."

But he hadn't said *leaving.* He'd said *if anything happened.* Was Cody sick? No. Cody was way too tough. And except for the limp, he was the picture of health. He couldn't be sick. He'd just misspoken.

Cody was healthy as a horse. He had to be. Because in spite of everything, she needed him to be.

She searched his gaze a few seconds longer. If he was sick, he wouldn't be itching to get back on the circuit. No. Cody was fine.

But he wasn't the type to think of giving up a dog he loved. Was he so worried about her working with cattle that he'd leave Oreo behind?

The bright September day had cooled to comfortable temperatures. Ally scanned the area to make sure all the animals were in the shade.

Sheltered by two huge live oaks, the petting zoo spread across the church lawn with various animals in the temporary pens Cody had built. Carnival game booths covered half of the parking lot, with horseback rides occupying the rest.

"This is the best petting zoo we've ever had." Caitlyn stroked a silver rabbit inside a pen. "I tried to get Ally to do this over the years on numerous occasions. She turned me down every time, but let Cody ask and here she is."

Under the guise of securing the goat's tether, Ally turned away to hide her heated cheeks. Was Caitlyn suspicious? She'd been studying Ally all afternoon. Had she figured out Ally had feelings for Cody?

"Cody didn't ask." Ally shot him a glare. "He signed

me up, leaving me little choice. Either do it or find someone else. It was easier to just do it."

"You signed her up?" Caitlyn frowned. "I thought you only suggested—"

"It worked out okay." Cody sent Caitlyn a panicked, wide-eyed "stop talking" look. "Dr. Bridges was able to fill in, your new vet tech is working this weekend, and when's the last time you took off?"

So he hadn't really signed her up. He'd only told her he had. She jabbed a finger at him. "Just don't try to make it an annual thing, buddy."

"I hated tricking you." He grimaced. "But it was for a good cause—to help the church and your furry friends. I hope you're not mad at me."

"I'm not." Ally managed to infuse lightheartedness into her voice. "But I'll be livid if you try something like that again." Though he'd probably be a memory by then.

"Maybe I'll have won you over with my charm by next year and you'll volunteer on your own."

"Uh, yeah, knock yourself out with that." Ally rolled her eyes, hoping to pull off the effortless friendly banter she and Cody once had. "Your charm bounces right off me." If only it were true. If only she could be immune to him.

"Kids should be getting home from school anytime." Caitlyn checked her watch. "Soon we'll be overrun. Are we ready?"

A car pulled into the lot, then another and another.

"Show's on." Ally stroked the horse's silky snout just as Cody patted her fingers instead of the horse.

Electricity shot up her arm and she snatched her hand away. Why had she agreed to this?

Because he'd gotten some of her pets adopted out and she felt she owed him?

No.

Because she wanted to find forever homes for more of her animals?

Partly.

But mostly because, try as she might, she couldn't resist Cody, and spending time with him was the highlight of her days. Even though he thought of her as only a friend. Even though she was happy on her own.

She was pathetic.

More arrivals, and in no time the parking lot teemed with vehicles and kids dragging their parents toward the games and zoo, along with a smattering of preteens trying to look bored.

"Wow, check him out." One of the girls giggled and elbowed her friend.

Ally's face heated. She knew who they were talking about without even looking.

Slade Walker and Mitch were helping with the horses and were both nice-looking men. But Cody drew females like a magnet.

Including her.

A day and a half spent with Cody. A beautiful kind of torture.

Half of day two at the petting zoo was behind them. Cody would go back to dropping in on Ally at her clinic, but this undivided time together would soon be over.

Truth be known, his cattle ranch bored him to tears— just as he suspected it would. But he had to make a living without the rodeo. Thankfully, he'd hired a great foreman and hands to run the place for him. Time with Ally was all that kept him sane.

He couldn't take his eyes off her as she helped a little girl hold a rabbit properly while the rest of the kids stood in a circle around her. So patient, so gentle with the children and the animals. Her smile went all the way to her eyes. Her laugh all the way to her heart.

"It's nice seeing her like that, huh?" Caitlyn squeezed his good shoulder. "The old Ally. I see glimmers of her every once in a while. Usually when she's with some critter."

"She used to be so much fun, so lighthearted and carefree. Now she's on edge."

His tone echoed his wistfulness for the old Ally.

"She changed after her dad died. If not for her vet practice, she'd probably be a hermit." Caitlyn brushed her hands down the front of her jeans, removing imaginary fur. "I'm truly amazed she agreed to help with the petting zoo. Usually I can't get her off her farm unless there's an animal needing treatment."

That was probably part of it. But Cody doubted she was tense with everyone the way she was with him. The kiss still hung between them.

"At least she still goes to church."

"Yeah, but something inside Ally died when her dad did."

"I shouldn't have left."

Caitlyn gave him a questioning look.

"I mean, her dad had just died." *Make it sound casual.* If Caitlyn figured out his feelings for Ally, she'd badger him to make a move. A move he had no right to make until he figured out what to do with his aneurysm. "I should have stuck around a little longer, put off my career for a while and supported my friend."

"She didn't want you to and if you had, she'd have pushed you away just like she did everyone else."

"How can we help her?"

"I think you moving in next door already has. You got her here. And no matter what she says, no one can resist your infectious charm for long." Caitlyn shot him a wink, patted his arm. "I better get back to horseback-riding duty. I just wanted to check and make sure you're not overdoing it on that leg."

"Ally ordered me to sit in this chair by the puppies and kittens, so that's what I'm doing. She handles the kids."

"Good." Caitlyn tousled his hair as if he were a child and turned toward the game area.

Ally caught him staring. Her smile died. The light in her eyes dimmed.

"Okay, kids." She clapped her hands to get their attention. "Let's go see the puppies and kittens over by Mr. Cody."

It would take much more than every ounce of charisma Cody could muster to crack the wall Ally had built around herself. And then he'd have to tread carefully on the friends-only path.

Invite the kids in for food, ply them with treats, then make them sit through a mini-sermon. They'd fallen for it both nights.

But Ally had seen through their plan. It was for the children and their parents. Not the workers.

In the church parking lot, dedicated members cleaned the game area, deflated the bouncy houses and picked up trash. She headed for the cattle trailer.

By the time parents and kids streamed out of the church, she'd loaded the horses, ponies and goats and hosed off the corner of the parking lot where the horses had been.

"There you are," Caitlyn called. "Mitch and some of the other guys could have done this."

"I know. But I'm used to it and I'm in charge of the animals."

"I'm glad to get a minute with you alone. Without Cody."

Ally's heart rattled. Caitlyn was on to her. She knew Ally was having a hard time resisting his appeal.

"Do you think he's okay?" Caitlyn asked.

Ally squelched a relieved sigh. This wasn't about her feelings for Cody. "You mean his injuries?"

"No. I mean his heart."

Oh, no. Had he just come off a bad relationship? *Please, Caitlyn, don't tell me about some woman in his life.*

"I know it must be hard for him to not rodeo anymore. He must be heartbroken." Caitlyn folded the chairs and leaned them against a tree.

Huh? So this wasn't about his love life. "I thought he decided not to go back."

"I can't imagine Cody deciding to quit, not as long as he's breathing. Don't you think it's strange that his sudden retirement came on the heels of his bull wreck?"

"You think he's hurt worse than he's letting on?" Ally's heart lodged in her throat.

"He's gotten a lot of concussions over the years."

"Maybe his doctor refused to release him."

"Don't tell him I said anything." Caitlyn rolled her eyes. "He tries to be all tough, you know."

Was Cody here only because he had to be? Grounded permanently? But even if he were banned from rodeo, that didn't mean he had to stay in Aubrey. He was only leasing.

More reason to stay away from him. He'd need a new diversion. Even if by some miracle Cody fell madly in love with her, she refused to be anybody's consolation prize. Especially not a temporary one.

"Speaking of Mr. Tough Guy," Caitlyn whispered.

The hair on the back of Ally's neck prickled.

"Where'd you go?" He limped toward her.

"I figured I'd get a head start out here." Was his limp permanent?

"It could've waited. We had six kids come forward."

"That's great." Her tone fell flat.

"Last night we had nine, for a total of fifteen. I wish some of the parents had gotten the message."

Why? So he could disappoint them, too?

"Are you okay?" Cody touched her arm.

"Fine." She took a step backward. "Just trying to get all these animals back to their homes." *And keep my distance. From you. And from God.*

"Once we get all the animals settled where they came from, all the carnival workers are meeting at Moms on Main for supper." Caitlyn strolled toward her car. "Want to join us, Ally?"

"I better get home."

"Oh, I forgot." Caitlyn checked her watch. "It's almost five and if you stay out past six—you turn into a goat."

"I do smell like one, but goats are cute." Ally folded her arms.

"Come on, Al." Cody sidled between the two women, slung his arms around each of their shoulders.

Ally's breath caught.

"You barely had any lunch." He gave her shoulder a squeeze. "You must be starving."

Why did his touch do things to her insides? Make her want to do his bidding? Her stomach growled.

Cody chuckled. "I'll take that as a yes."

"I guess I am kind of famished." Ally patted her tummy, willing it to silence. "But didn't y'all eat with the kids?"

"I saved my appetite for Moms." Caitlyn brushed off her jeans.

"I did eat a PB&J sandwich." Cody gave her a sheepish grin. "But I consider it an appetizer."

She really should just go home and stay away from Cody. But her mother had book club tonight and Ally didn't relish the concept of heading to an empty house. "I'll get the critters settled and see y'all there."

"We're shooting for seven." Cody finally moved his arm. "That'll give everybody a couple of hours. Caitlyn should have plenty of time to get rid of her horsiness."

"I wouldn't be talking." Caitlyn picked cat fur off his sleeve as her mischievous grin slipped into place.

They separated then, going to their respective vehicles. The three of them—like old times. Ally had missed them. Except her heart couldn't conjure up her past friendly feelings for Cody. It wanted much more.

Chapter Six

Why had Cody suggested he ride with Ally to Moms? He needed to keep her at a distance. Being in the same truck hadn't helped his resolve. Neither did sitting beside her at the long table.

He polished off his cheeseburger and tried to concentrate on what Pastor Thomas was saying.

"We got names and addresses for the kids who came forward each day?" The pastor squirted another blob of ketchup on his plate.

"We did." Mitch folded his napkin, pushed his plate away. "We'll invite the parents to church or see if the kids want to ride the bus."

"Definitely," Pastor Thomas agreed. "I've been going through our files, too, checking on members we haven't seen in a while."

"Ally used to be a member," Cody said, then popped a fry in his mouth.

Ally set her tea down with a thunk. Her face pinkened. "I'm a member of a church in Denton now."

"As long as you're going somewhere." The pastor gave her a genuine smile.

Something caught her attention and her eyes widened.

Cody followed her gaze toward the end of the long table. Her mom and Dr. Bridges laughing and talking as they searched for a table. Coworkers sharing supper? Maybe, but Diane's hand rested in the crook of Dr. Bridges's arm. On a Saturday night? With him wearing slacks and a button-down and her in a dress? Still could be a coworker thing. He glanced back at Ally. Not from the look of shock on her face.

"Well, this preacher needs to get some sleep if I intend to deliver a lucid sermon in the morning." Pastor Thomas pushed his chair back and laid several bills on the table for their server.

The rest of the gathering contributed to the tip, stood and strolled toward the exit.

Surprise spread over her mom's features as she saw them. "Ally?" Her hand jerked away from Dr. Bridges's arm. Color flushed her cheeks. "Lance—um, Dr. Bridges—and I just decided to stop in for pie and coffee after our dinner."

"They have really good pie here." Cody tried to ease the tension, but it swirled thick around them. "But not as good as Miss Diane's four-layer delight."

"Are you hinting for another?" Her mom smiled. "I'll be home shortly, Al."

"See you then." Ally leveled a look at Dr. Bridges. "Shortly."

Obviously upset. Cody pressed his hand to the small of her back to get her moving, then opened the door for her. Maybe it was a good thing they'd ridden together after all.

"I can't believe my mom is dating." A pent-up wail escaped from Ally as soon as Cody shut his truck door.

"You think it was a date?"

"Hello? It's Saturday night. Did you see what they were

wearing? She admitted they'd been out for dinner. And they were all cozy." She let out a world-weary sigh.

"I thought you liked Lance."

"I do. But she's my mom." She started the engine, pulled out of the parking space. "I know it's been twelve years since my dad…and I should be happy for her. Her life basically stopped when Dad's did. But…"

"It's hard seeing your mom with somebody other than your dad." He covered her free hand with his.

"I'm acting like a preteen. How did you know how I'm feeling?" she sputtered.

"Grandpa's seeing someone. I met her when I stayed with him in Medina. It's been almost thirteen years since Grandma died. But seeing him with this new woman—it didn't settle well at first."

"I remember how broken he was when your grandmother died." Six months before her dad. And her parents had let her go to Medina for the funeral. She'd hugged Cody for the first time. With that hug, a barrier between them had slipped away. Or at least it had for her. "You got used to him having someone new?"

"Had to."

"Do you like her?"

"She's a right fine lady. Been good for him. But I had to get past my awkwardness to see that."

"How'd you do that?"

"I consciously listed all the good things I knew about her and then I prayed about it." He turned toward her. "So what do you know about Dr. Lance Bridges?"

"He lives in Denton and started coming to our church after his wife died of cancer about two and a half years ago. They'd attended where they were married and he couldn't bring himself to go there after her death." She pulled into her drive and cut the engine.

Cody got out, came around and opened her door.

She climbed out, leaned against the truck. With him beside her. Familiar and comforting, his arm against hers.

"What about his veterinary practice?"

"It was at their house and his wife helped with the office work. I think the memories got to him, so it was overwhelming after she died. He sold and moved to a smaller house. But he was at loose ends, so I hired him to work for me. He's planning to work a few more years and then retire."

"Nothing bad?"

"Nothing other than he's dating my mom. And I shouldn't see that as a bad thing."

"Pray on it." His hand clasped hers. "I'll pray for you, too."

"Thanks." Warmth threaded through her, along with unease over more than her mom.

He patted his shoulder. "Need this?"

She shouldn't. She really shouldn't. But she did.

"I've really missed you." She turned into him, resting her cheek against his chest. His arms came around her, gentle, soothing. A contented sigh escaped. Cody's embrace was like home. "I mean your friendship. Your nonjudgmental ear."

"Glad to be of use and right back at you." His voice rumbled against her ear. "Dear Lord, help Ally to cope with her mom dating Lance. If they're meant to be, let Lance be the man Diane needs and ease Ally's discomfort over the whole deal. If there's someone else in Diane's future, You know who he is. Whatever the future holds for Diane and for Ally, give them both peace. Thank You for all the blessings You give us. Amen."

No man had ever prayed for her. Except her dad. Even though she'd quit putting any stock in prayer a long time ago, Cody's sincere gesture liquefied her heart further. He gave her an extra squeeze and Ally was certain she'd never be able to pry herself away from him.

"Hey, I've been thinking." He propped his chin on her head. "We should put together a float for your shelter in the Peanut Festival parade."

"A float?"

"Maybe a Noah's ark theme with animals everywhere. It would be great advertisement. Might get some adoptions out of it."

"Noah's ark with cats and dogs only?" The throb of his heart, strong and steady against her ear. How could he be so calm, when her heart was racing?

"Well, yeah. But it fits the concept. The ark saved Noah's family and the animals. Our ark will save cats and dogs. I'll find a way to make it work."

"That's actually a good idea. But I don't know a thing about floats."

"I can figure it out. Build a cardboard frame shaped like a boat, cut windows for the cages to show through."

"It's only a few weeks away."

"It won't take long." He rubbed calming circles on her back. "I'll do the building. If you help paint in the evenings when you finish work, we can knock it out in no time."

"I don't have a trailer."

"I do."

"I can't ask you to do this. You already help so much with my animals."

"You're not asking. I offered. And to be honest, I'm feeling kind of useless."

If he felt useless was wanderlust taking hold? "What about your ranch?"

"I've figured out ranching isn't really my thing. My foreman and hands do all the work."

Bored already. He probably wouldn't stick around much longer.

"If it doesn't come together as fast as we need, I can put some of my hands to work on it, too."

"There's no need for that."

"Whatever you need, I'll do. I'd do anything for you, Ally—don't you know that by now?"

Anything except stay. Anything except love her.

But she didn't want him to anyway. She didn't.

Her eyes flew open as an engine sounded and head-lights panned over them.

"They're back." Ally jerked away from him. "I can't face her right now." She barreled toward the house and scurried inside. Already showered, she didn't even stop to let the dogs out of the mudroom. She went straight to her room and pulled out her jammies. By the time Mom got inside, Ally planned to be in bed. No heart-to-hearts over Mom's new beau. Ally couldn't take it.

As she settled, switched off the lamp, Lance's engine started, then faded away.

Foxy's and Wolf's nails clicked across the living room floor.

Mom's shadow darkened her doorway. "It's not what you think. Lance and I are only friends, coworkers."

"It's fine. I'm just tired from wrangling all the animals at the carnival."

A pause. "Goodnight, then." Mom's silhouette drifted away.

Ally had worked with Lance for two years. All the times Mom had invited him to stay for supper, the times they'd shared a laugh in the clinic, drunk a cup of coffee in the break room or worried over an animal together. Why hadn't Ally seen them growing closer?

Because she hadn't wanted to.

Her stomach churned. But even worse than the upset over Mom and Lance was the disquiet of how good Cody's comfort tonight had felt.

"Ally?" Cody rapped his knuckles against her childhood bedroom window. Had she changed rooms?

A light came on, and the curtain was pushed aside. Her face in the window—squinted eyes. "What are you doing?"

"Your critters are loose again."

"Oh, no." The curtains swooshed closed.

"I called Mitch to help."

"Thanks. I'll be right out," she shouted.

Cody had been consistently using his newly purchased treadmill to strengthen his knee. This time he wouldn't sit back in the barn. This time he'd rustle animals. The barn door was open and by the time she stepped out on her back porch, Cody had a handful of leashes.

"Thanks." She grabbed several from him as headlights pulled into the drive.

A truck door slammed. "Don't touch any doorknobs or latches," Mitch called. "Maybe I can get some prints this time."

Ally whirled around to face Cody. "You called him in Texas Ranger mode?"

"It's the second time, Ally. I don't think you can handle this on your own." Cody hobbled after a Lab mix, clicking his tongue, baby-talking until the dog came to him. He slipped the collar in place. "Where does this one go? Barn or clinic?"

"Barn." She vaulted toward the open door of the clinic. "This can't get out. It could ruin my business. Get my shelter shut down."

"We use discretion with all our investigations." Mitch's flashlight cut through the darkness as he followed after her. "But if it'll make you feel better, I'll file it under un-official business. Helping out a friend. I'm even off duty for a couple of days."

"I like that second option. Tell your brother to stay in the barn. I don't want him hurting himself."

"I'm fine." Cody steered the large dog into the barn. He elbowed the door shut and latched it, then shone his beam over the property. A flash of white. "Oreo, is that you?"

The dog bounded toward him, wagging his tail.

"You better not run off, boy." He slid the collar over the dog's head and made another trip to the barn. "We need to know how many."

"I'm on it." Ally jogged toward the clinic.

The back door of her house opened and her mom stepped out on the lit porch. "I called Lance. He should be here any minute."

Ally's heavy sigh echoed through the darkness. Already upset over the situation with her mom and Lance, and now her animals being loose again added more stress. Whoever did this, Cody would gladly ring their neck. But right now he needed to rustle up the critters. And keep Ally safe.

Hours later, with the first rays of daylight, Ally gently set the last kitten in her cage.

"That's all of them?" Cody shuffled into Oreo's pen and settled in a folding chair.

"Yes. Thankfully, it wasn't as bad this time." She swiped her wrist over her temple, pushing sweat-soaked hair away from her face. "Only eight dogs and eleven cats this time."

"But one of 'em was Oreo. That makes this personal."

"Either of you notice anything suspicious lately?" Mitch leaned against the wall.

"I really don't think this is necessary." Ally shook her head. "I'll change the locks. It'll be fine."

"If this was the first time, I might be inclined to let it slide. But twice? Whoever we're dealing with obviously has no concern for your four-legged friends' safety. If somebody wants to shut you down, they might not be above hurting the animals."

Ally gasped. "I hadn't thought about that."

"Or hurting Ally." Cody's low tone sent a shiver over her.

Or Mom. The magnitude of the situation twisted her insides.

"I got several partial latent prints off the barn door latch, the clinic knob and the cage bolts. I got your mom's, Lance's and Cody's prints already. Once I get yours and Derek's, I'll know which ones can be ruled out. Anybody else I need to exclude?"

"About a dozen volunteers from church come each evening, but I need this to stay quiet."

"I'll show up tomorrow and explain there's some new state regulation that requires all volunteers' prints on file."

"Trick them?" Ally's shoulders sagged.

"Either that or come clean. I'll let you decide. Anyone else?"

"My state inspector was here last week." Her eyes squeezed shut. "But you can't contact him for information or prints. If he finds out about this, he'll write me up and could shut me down. And if you're right, whoever is doing this would win."

"I see." Mitch made a note on his pad. "Anybody got a bone to pick with you?"

"Not that I can think of."

"What about your employees, Cody? Any of them complain about the noise level of the shelter getting on their nerves?"

"No." Cody scratched Oreo's neck. With a contented sigh, the dog set his head on Cody's knee. "In fact, they're all animal lovers and most have mentioned what a good program Ally runs."

"Anything odd other than the loose animals?"

"The inspector only comes once a year and he'd already been here back in the spring." Ally sank onto a hay bale. "For him to come again, someone had to file a complaint. But again, you can't contact him and grievances are usually anonymous, so he wouldn't tell you anyway."

"Maybe something will turn up with the prints." Mitch closed his notepad. "You let me know if anything else happens. I mean it, Ally. I'm on your side. And the most important thing is to keep you and the animals safe."

She nodded, swallowed hard. Could Mitch be right? Could her nemesis be willing to hurt the animals? Or Mom?

"What about patrolling the area at night?" Cody's chair moaned as he stood.

"That wouldn't be a problem, since I'm right down the road anyway." Mitch made another note.

"No, Mitch, I can't let you do that." Ally hung her head. "You've got Caitlyn and your baby girl. I can't drag you away from them every night."

"Actually, I meant me." Cody stepped out of Oreo's pen, paced between the kennels. "I don't have a schedule or a family. I could camp out in the barn at night. Or the clinic."

"Absolutely not." Mitch adjusted his cowboy hat. "What if our interloper is armed? If anybody does any staking out, it'll be an officer. How many nights between incidents?"

"About a week. The first time was on a Saturday morning. This time it's Sunday."

"Maybe a nine-to-fiver who doesn't work weekends or someone who works the evening shift. I'll see what I can arrange with the department and keep you posted." Mitch headed for the door.

"Let me sleep on your couch." Cody hung the last leash back in place and turned to Ally.

"No."

"You and your mom—two women alone in a house—with someone up to no good creeping around outside."

"But nothing's been toward me." She stood, hugged herself. "Just the animals."

"Yes, but letting the animals out hasn't gotten our perp anywhere. Both times we wrangled them all back with no one the wiser. Chaotic and problematic, but not conducive to shutting you down. He might go after you the next time. Or your mom."

No fair bringing her mom into this. Her insides gave another turn. "Those are mighty big words for a cowboy."

"Stop trying to use humor as a cover. I can see it in your eyes—you're scared." He stepped close, his breath fanning her temple.

So close. So tempting. His broad shoulder just waiting for her to snuggle in.

Chapter Seven

Ally buried her face in his chest. A shudder moved through her.

His arms surrounded her. Safety and peril in one muscled package.

"I'm sleeping on your couch. Until this is over. Period. I'd rather have you safe than me be sorry."

Slowly going crazy in his embrace. Having Cody next door was way too close for comfort. Having him on her couch was insane. She wouldn't sleep a wink.

"No." She pulled away from him. "They won't come back tonight and I'll have the locks changed tomorrow."

"Fine, Miss Independent." He ran his hand over the back of his neck. "I'll change the locks for you. First thing."

"I can hire someone."

"I'll do it."

"Okay." Whatever it took to keep him off her couch. At a nice safe distance. "You're way too serious these days. Whatever happened to fun-loving Cody?"

"I'm too worried for fun." He shoved his hands in his pockets.

"But you used to be the one to crack a joke when life

got too intense." She shrugged one shoulder. "I miss your sense of humor."

"Really." He ducked his head. "All this time, I've been biting my tongue, trying to act more mature."

"Why?"

"So everyone will take me seriously."

"The world is way too grim as it is. We need more Cody—not less. You're perfect just the way you are." She bit her lip, wishing she could stuff the words back in. "Or the way you were."

"Well, in that case, did you hear about the cowboy adopting the dachshund?"

"No." She grinned, anticipating something corny.

"He wanted to get a long little doggy."

She shook her head, started for her house.

"Hey, I thought you'd like that one, being a vet and all." He fell in stride beside her, exited the barn and checked the latch. "Where are you going? I've got a zillion more packed inside me like tennis balls in a Lab's mouth."

"I said I missed your humor. Not your corny jokes."

"I'm rusty. Just give me a minute."

"Maybe your brain will fire better after you get some sleep." She climbed her porch steps.

"Lock up." All humor died in his eyes. "I've half a mind to stay with you despite your protests."

"We'll be fine. Thanks for your help. Get some rest." *Let me breathe.*

"I'm not leaving until I hear the dead bolt."

She dragged her gaze away from his magnetic pull and stepped inside. With a metallic click, the dead bolt slid into place, and his footfalls descended the porch. She leaned back against the door.

But even with the distance between them, she still couldn't breathe right.

* * *

Coffee. Cody inhaled, savoring the rich scent. Whoever came up with the concept of the automatic timer on coffeemakers deserved to be a millionaire. Even though it was decaf. He opened his eyes to the bright sunshine. As he stretched, the previous night came back to him.

Ally's animals loose again. They'd worked a good five hours rounding them up.

After he'd seen Ally safely to her house, he'd showered, and since Jackie's Hardware was closed on Sundays, he'd driven to Denton, then returned and changed the locks on Ally's house, clinic and barn. He'd sorely wanted to go to morning service, but after all that, his eyes wouldn't stay open and he'd conked out in the recliner.

Another stretch and he peered at the clock. Almost twelve thirty. He sat up, rubbed his eyes. When was the last time he'd missed church? He'd definitely go tonight.

Coffee. Even if it was fake. He headed toward the kitchen.

A scream pierced the quiet.

Ally?

Cody bolted outside.

Over in front of her truck, Ally backed away with both hands over her mouth.

"What's wrong?" He ran to her.

Her hand shook as she pointed at the windshield.

DIE! A single word scrawled in soap.

A chill crawled up his spine. He stepped in front of her, scanned the property. "Get inside."

The threat had probably been left last night, but just in case.

"But I have a wedding to go to."

"I think you should sit this one out."

"I can't. I'm a bridesmaid."

His brain cleared enough to take in her long burgundy

dress. Her dark hair in waves, loose and cascading around her shoulders.

It did something funny to his breathing. "Whose wedding?"

"My cousin Landry and I can't let her down." She checked her watch. "It's at two at the Ever After Chapel."

"Oh, yeah. I was traveling, but she included me in Mitch's invitation." He shifted his weight from one foot to the other. "I'd feel better about things if you didn't go alone today."

"Well, you're not dressed appropriately." Her gaze skimmed over his typical jeans, Western shirt and boots.

"Go inside and give me five minutes." He fished his phone from his pocket. "I'll call Mitch and we'll take my truck so he can check yours for prints."

"Come on, Cody—I don't need a babysitter." She stamped her foot. "It's a wedding. You think some nut's going to attack me?"

"Mitch said to keep an eye on you. Go back inside. I'll be over in a jiff."

"This is ridiculous," she huffed, but turned back toward her house. "You can't babysit me 24/7."

No. But he could make sure she stayed out of trouble today. And appreciate her beauty while he was at it. He made his way inside.

If only he could talk Ally out of going to the wedding. But he knew Landry and Ally had always been close—graduating only a few years apart. He wouldn't be able to convince her not to go.

What kind of person skulked around in darkness letting animals loose and wreaking havoc, leaving threatening notes on windshields? With soap? Maybe teens pulling pranks? He hoped so. But his twisting gut said Ally was in danger. And he wouldn't let anything happen to her.

* * *

"Do you really think it's a good idea to go to the wedding?" Mom wrung her hands.

"I can't let Landry down." Ally willed her shaking to stop. "I'll be fine. Cody's going with me."

"Oh, good." The lines between Mom's eyebrows relaxed.

"Why don't you come, too? I know you said you wanted to leave a little later, but obviously, I'm not going as early as I planned. Mitch should be here any minute, but until he arrives, I'm not sure I like the idea of you being here alone."

"Lance is taking me to the wedding. But I'm concerned about no one being home with everything going on."

"Oh." Torn. Lance escorting her mom would ease Ally's worries. And worsen them. "I'll ask Cody to get one of his hands to come over and keep an eye on things."

A knock sounded and Ally jumped.

"It's me, Cody."

Breathe in, breathe out. Calm down. She unlocked the extra dead bolt he'd installed that morning, opened the door.

Handsome in a gray suit with a burgundy shirt and paisley undone tie to match. He pointed at it. "I tried three times. Can you help?"

"Sure." She adjusted the ends to the right length, looped it over. "We're worried about no one being here this afternoon. Do you think one of your hands could keep an eye on things?"

"I already arranged it." His breath fanned her hair.

"Thanks." A tremble inched over her. She chanced a glance at him. His gaze was riveted on hers. Too close. She tugged the tie into place, tightened the knot.

Cody's hands covered hers. "You trying to choke me?"

"Sorry."

"You two look like a couple." Mom clapped her hands. Heat swept up Ally's neck.

"I thought we should look like we'd planned to attend together all along so if our perp happens to be watching, it doesn't look like he's got Ally running scared."

"Good thinking." Ally checked her watch. "We need to go."

"Mitch was pulling in just as I knocked."

"And Lance will be here any minute." Mom peered out the window. "You two go. Forget all this nonsense. And I'll see you in a bit."

Cody held the door open for her and she stepped out.

Mitch and another officer combed over her truck.

"What happened to off-the-record favor for a friend?" she whispered.

"There's been a threat now, Ally. It has to become official. But don't worry—they'll keep it quiet." Cody's hand pressed against the small of her back.

Too familiar. Too comforting. She stiffened.

"You're a bundle of nerves."

"I can't help it. I've got a few things on my mind."

He escorted her to the driver's side of his truck. "You'll have to drive. My doc is still being overly cautious with my knee and hasn't released me to drive."

It was no easy task to climb into the truck wearing the dress, but she managed. Cody shut her door, rounded to the passenger's side and eased in.

"Thanks." She could feel his stare as she started the engine and pulled onto the highway. Kept her eyes on the yellow line.

"I don't think I've ever seen you so dressed up."

"Good?" Her skin heated. "Or bad?"

"You look great."

"Really?" She smoothed a shaky hand over her skirt.

"It's just so different than what I'm used to wearing. I had to practice how to walk for days in these shoes." The strappy high heels matched her dress perfectly, but they definitely weren't built for comfort.

"Who's Landry marrying?"

"Kyle Billings. He's not from around here."

"Ever wonder if you made the right decision to stay single?"

Only since he came back to town. "No. You?"

"I'm not sure anymore."

Her breath hitched.

"I mean, it might be nice to have somebody to share things with. Triumphs, trials, health issues."

"I share all that with my mom." And it had been enough. Until Cody came back.

"Yeah, but if your mom gets serious with Lance? What then?"

"I'll still share my triumphs and trials with her." And she was hoping her mom and Lance wouldn't get more serious. It might make work uncomfortable if they ended things, but Ally's life would get back to normal. Wasn't that completely selfish. "I'm not thirty yet. Surely I've got lots of time before any health issues kick in."

"You never know. But then, burdening somebody else with your health issues doesn't seem right."

"It's marriage." Ally shrugged, trying to feel as indifferent as she sounded. "I guess if two people love each other enough to commit their lives to one another, they're willing to face anything and everything together."

"Ever wonder if we're missing out on that?"

"Tell you what—stick around in Aubrey and when we get old and decrepit, I'll drive you to doctor's appointments and you can haul me to the hospital when I need to go."

"I may just hold you to that." His hand covered her free

one, twining their fingers. And it felt way too good. Way too warm. Way too dizzying.

But she knew he wouldn't hold her to her pledge. Because he'd never stick around that long.

Still breathing odd, Cody escorted Ally into the Ever After Chapel.

"Ally. Bridesmaids in here." Landry's mom pulled her away from him. "Cody, nice to see you."

"You, too, Mrs. Malone."

"See you after the ceremony." Ally waved her fingers at him.

The two women disappeared into a side room. Alone, Cody concentrated on normal breathing. Someone poked him in the ribs and he flinched.

"Did I just see you walk in with Ally?" Raquel, his friend and neighbor from several acres away, was downright giddy.

"Yeah? So?" He looked to her husband for clarification, but Slade only smirked.

"What?"

"You really don't remember, do you?" Raquel's smug smile confused him further.

"Remember what?"

"When you were in the hospital after your bull wreck and I came to visit you, we were talking about that time Mitch tried to fix us up but we were destined to only be friends."

"So?"

"So, you said you wished we could pick who we fall for and then you said you were in love with Ally."

Cody's eyes widened. His heart went into overdrive. "I did not."

"Yes, you did." She rolled her eyes. "That's why I

came up with the whole pet visitation program to the rehab center—to get her there to see you." She shrugged. "I mean, I wanted to help patients and help Ally's strays, too, but the idea came to me because of you."

Slade chuckled. "Looks like your devious plan worked. I'm glad Mitch's fix-up didn't and I won the prize." He pulled Raquel against his side.

"Ally and I are friends. That's all." Cody lowered his voice. "She had another break-in at the clinic. I'm worried someone's out to get her, so I didn't think she should come to this wedding alone."

"Well, I hate to hear about her problems at the clinic. But you want to protect her because you love her." Raquel jabbed a finger at him. "You can deny it all you want, but I heard what I heard."

He couldn't have said he loved Ally all those months ago. He hadn't even known it then. There had to be an explanation. Raquel must have misunderstood him. Or maybe the medication had affected him.

"Was I on pain meds when I supposedly made this confession?"

"Well...yeah." Raquel raised one shoulder. "But I used to be an emergency room nurse. Sometimes medication brings out the truth."

"Just do me a favor—keep my drug-induced declaration to yourself, will ya?"

"Of course." Raquel covered her mouth with her hand and winked. "You should be the one to tell her."

"Come on—leave the man in peace." Slade tugged her toward the door to the chapel.

"You coming?" Raquel called over her shoulder.

"I'll wait on Mitch. He's bachin' it, too, since Caitlyn's in the wedding party. I'll be there in a bit."

The open door gave him a glimpse of more lace and filmy fabric than he'd ever seen flanking the old-fashioned pews.

Had he really said he loved Ally back in the hospital? Had his heart known what his head refused to admit?

Why did he have such horrible timing? Why couldn't he have realized his feelings back when he'd kissed her? Why couldn't he have stuck around to figure it out instead of running scared to the rodeo?

They could have had a chance. Back when he was healthy. Back when his future was endless. He'd have quit the rodeo for her. Never gotten injured. Never been ruled by a time bomb in his head.

So many regrets. But Ally topped the list.

He let out a harsh breath as Mitch stepped inside.

"Hey, little brother."

"Did you get any prints off Ally's truck?"

"A few partials. We'll have to do a comparison with the ones from the other night."

"Any leads?"

Several guests entered the foyer and Mitch waited until they were out of earshot. "The prints from the barn and clinic doors didn't match anything in our database, so our perp has no prior record."

"What now?"

"Patience. You just concentrate on keeping an eye on Ally. But I did learn something you might be interested in."

"What?"

"Garrett Steele is opening a bull-riding school in Aubrey. Thought you might be interested in applying as an instructor."

Adrenaline rushed through Cody. For the first time since his injuries, he was excited over something other than Ally.

* * *

The leather interior of Cody's truck still had that new-car smell. He'd always treated his vehicles like his babies. Probably had it detailed once a week.

"I can't believe this." Ally sniffled as she drove.

"You okay?"

"I just feel so bad for Landry. How could her fiancé leave her at the altar? I mean, if you want to call the wedding off, do it before everybody shows up."

"I'd like to put a burr under his saddle." Cody handed her a tissue.

She dabbed her nose. "I thought stuff like this only happened in movies."

"It's good she found out he wasn't the type to stick around before she married him." Cody adjusted his seat belt looser on his injured shoulder. "Where'd she meet the good-for-nothing?"

"He was a guest at your cousin's dude ranch."

"Wow. I'm surprised she still works there after all these years. She always wanted to own her own ranch. I guess I figured she would by now."

"That's what makes it even worse." Ally swabbed under her eyes with her thumb. Probably looked like a raccoon, but seeing her younger cousin so shattered put an ache in her soul. "She and her fiancé planned to buy a bed-and-breakfast in Denton."

"I'm getting madder by the mile."

"It just proves we're not missing out on a thing by staying single." She gripped the steering wheel tighter, turning her knuckles white, wishing it were her cousin's ex's neck.

"That's a blanket statement. I've never heard of this happening in real life before."

"No. But if the wedding actually happens, so many

couples end up divorced. And if they stay married, one up and dies."

"Not always." He placed his hand on hers, gave a squeeze. "Both my folks are still kicking. There are several young couples I know who are still going strong. Widows who remarried like Raquel. Even your mom finally seems to be moving on. And lots of folks are still married into their golden years."

"But the uncertainty of it makes it not worth bothering with."

"You really believe that?"

"More and more every day." Especially when Cody compromised her determination for independence. Time to change the subject. "You and Garrett seemed deep in conversation before we left." She pulled into his drive, parked and faced him.

"I got a job." Enthusiasm sparkled in his eyes.

Something she hadn't seen since he'd been home. "What kind of job?"

"An instructor at Garrett's new bull-riding school."

"What?" A vein in her neck throbbed. "How could you do something so stupid! You're barely walking, you can't drive, it's a wonder you're alive, and you're going right back in the arena."

"I'm—"

"I can't believe you." She jerked the door open and climbed down.

Gravel scattered as Cody scrambled to catch up with her as she stalked toward her house. "Ally, I—"

"That you'd torment your family all over again." She wheeled around toward him. "That you'd put me through worrying about you. You barely survived your last bull wreck. Why do you always have to push the limits?"

"You're concerned about me?" A cocky smile settled into place.

And her arteries went hot lava. "Of course I am, you idiot. Why wouldn't I be when you insist on cavorting around on the backs of mammoth beasts who'd just as soon kill you as look at you?" She spun away from him and started for her porch.

"Ally, wait." His hand caught her wrist.

"What?" She stopped, rather than dragging him along limp and all, but kept her back to him, terrified the tears forming in her eyes might spill. She'd expected Cody to go back to the rodeo. But she'd never thought about how much his riding again would petrify her.

"I won't be riding."

The dread in her chest eased up. "How can you teach bull riding and not ride?"

"I'll review videos of professional riders with students and explain technique. I'll give advice while they practice on a stationary bull and then graduate to real bulls. But my feet stay outside the arena the entire time."

Relief sucked her lungs empty. She blinked several times and turned around. "Oh. Guess I overreacted."

His smile widened. As if he was onto her.

Had she revealed her feelings?

"It's almost time for evening church." She hurried the rest of the way to her door.

Even if she'd let her feelings show, he wasn't interested.

Even if he were, she had to get a handle on this. She could never take the chance of someone leaving her at the altar. Or cheating on her. Or dying on her. She couldn't allow herself to need Cody. Or anybody else.

Chapter Eight

Barren hay fields surrounded the house and barn. Ally moved her stethoscope over the creamy horse's chest.

A typical Monday. Lots of sick pets. Nothing serious. No loose animals. No strays. No surprise inspections. Finishing up with a house call. All in all, a good day.

"Have you seen poor Landry since the almost wedding?" Raquel's sympathetic tone interrupted the steady *whump whump, whump whump* of the horse's heart.

"No. I called to check on her, but my aunt said she didn't feel like talking."

"Poor girl. Hunter's dad and I stayed at the dude ranch years ago and I've gotten reacquainted with her since moving to Aubrey."

"Landry has lots of people to love her through this." Ally removed her stethoscope and stroked the mare's velvety neck. "This one's strong and healthy as a horse."

"That's what I'm afraid of." Raquel blew out a sigh. "Why couldn't Slade have gotten Hunter a pony for his birthday? I mean, every kid wants a pony. Not a full-grown—way-too-tall—horse."

"You can't tell me—" Ally pointed to the weathered gray barn behind Raquel's house "—you don't realize that barn and pasture are crying out for a horse. This is Aubrey, Texas. I'm surprised it's even legal to live here and not own a horse."

"But Hunter's only eight."

Ally's humor fell flat in the face of a mother's anxieties.

"She's a nice horse." Ally checked the palomino's teeth. "Gentle and she doesn't spook. She barely even flinched when I vaccinated her."

"She's just so big." Raquel shivered. "It's a long way to the ground from up there."

"Hunter will be fine. Has he ever ridden before?"

"Not alone."

"One of my clients gives riding lessons. I'm sure she could teach Hunter. And maybe you, too." Ally patted the horse's shoulder. "Maybe if you learn to ride, you'll feel better about Hunter riding."

"I already made arrangements for lessons. Wait—how did you know I don't ride?"

"Um…you cringe every time the mare moves."

"Okay, I admit it—I'm afraid of horses." Raquel covered her face with both hands. "And I live in Horse Country, USA. Is there a support group for that?"

"Admitting it is the first step." Ally laughed.

"Thanks for coming over here."

"No problem. When the horse is five minutes away, it just doesn't make sense for y'all to load her in a trailer and bring her over to my place."

"I'm surprised you have time for house calls." Raquel handed her a check. "Are you still doing the hospital and rehab visits with the dogs?"

"I am." Ally stroked the horse's silken muzzle. "Thanks for coming up with that. I've adopted a dozen or so dogs out and the patients love the visits."

"Now that we've settled into newlywed bliss, I'll volunteer to help again soon."

"That would be great. I've gotten a few volunteers signed up, but the more, the better."

"I noticed you and Cody attended the wedding that wasn't. Together."

"We didn't plan to. It just worked out that way."

"He told me about the second break-in." The horse swatted its tail and Raquel flinched. "Don't worry—I won't say a word. But have you ever thought of dating Cody?"

Ally's breathing stuttered. "I've known him forever. Back in high school, he was the brother I never had."

"Back in high school." Raquel's brows lifted. "But what about now?"

"We're friends. Neighbors. That's all." Ally put her supplies back in her bag.

A truck pulled into the drive at the front of the house.

"Here's Hunter and Slade. They went to buy a saddle." Raquel shook her head. "Who buys a horse when they don't even own a saddle?" But when her smile landed on Slade, Ally could see that all her frustration over the horse melted away.

"Tell them I said hey." Ally waved to the man and boy and headed for her truck. To go home. Alone.

She placed her supplies back in the mobile clinic in her truck bed, then climbed in the cab. The engine purred to life and she backed out of the barn lot onto the highway.

No, she wasn't alone. She had a plethora of stray dogs and cats to keep her company, plus a few furry friends of her own. Though now that Mom's relationship with Lance was out in the open, Mom hadn't been home as much. She was losing the one person she could talk to at home.

Truth be told, she'd been lonely for years. Even living

with Mom. But it was even worse with Lance in Mom's picture. Nothing was the same. Ally liked Lance. He was a nice man, a conscientious vet, and he treated her mother well. But he wasn't Dad.

And Raquel's happiness put an ache in Ally's heart. A longing for her own romance. Her own forever after with Cody.

Her road appeared. Almost home and she didn't even remember the drive there.

Stop thinking about him that way. He was already obviously bored playing ranch. How long before he got bored teaching bull riding? It was only a matter of time before he'd be raring to get back on the road. She needed to remind herself often of Landry's attempt at happily-ever-after.

Her phone rang as she exited her truck. She dug it out of her pocket. "Hello?"

Silence. The uncomfortable sensation of someone watching her. She scanned her property.

"Hey." Cody on his side of the fence, holding his phone up. "It was me calling, but I saw you pull up, so I figured we'd talk in person."

"About?" She tried for a casual tone. Didn't quite pull it off.

"If we're gonna build a float, we need to git 'er done. It's almost the middle of September already, less than three weeks away from the parade. I've been researching and figured out the design. Feel like coming over to talk about it?"

How could she not think about Cody if he kept popping up with one idea or another? And now they were going to work on a float together? But her participation in the parade would help her animals.

"Sure. Let me get cleaned up a bit and I'll be right over."

How could she say no? She'd just have to pull up her big-girl boots, concentrate on her strays—not Cody—and get the job done.

Cardboard and two-by-fours surrounded Cody on the hay-strewn floor of his barn. He'd almost tripped once already. Had he bitten off more than he could chew? No. Not for Ally. He'd do anything for her. He'd even told her so. She'd figure him out—his iffy health and how he felt about her—if he didn't keep his guard up better.

Not in all his almost thirty years had he ever built a float. But he'd found help on the internet and managed to cut the cardboard into a pretty convincing ark shape. All he had to do was build a frame, staple the cardboard to it, and work out where to cut windows and how to stack the kennels without endangering any animals. That was where Ally would come in.

"Wow. I thought we were just going to talk about it." Ally. Behind him.

He turned to face her. "We don't have any time to waste."

"How did you come up with all this?"

"YouTube."

"I'm impressed." She held the frame for him as he used his nail gun. "Where did you get such huge sheets of cardboard?"

"There's a manufacturer in Fort Worth. One of my hands was going there anyway for ranch supplies."

"How much do I owe you?"

"Consider it my contribution to your shelter. All I require in return is some work and sweat. I need your brainpower on where to put the windows and how to stabilize the cages in place." He finished securing the cardboard and she stepped away.

Hands on hips, she strolled around the supplies a few times, then tapped her chin with a forefinger. "We can put the smaller animals higher up. Maybe stack hay bales for support and build a shelf between the beams where the cages will sit."

"I knew you'd figure it out." He started the next side of the frame and again she held it for him.

"Did I tell you about my big event this Saturday?"

"I saw a flyer on the bulletin board at church. Something about people getting pictures with their pets and a concert featuring Aubrey's own Garrett Steele and Brant McConnell."

"Kendra came up with it months ago." She waited while he sank three more nails. "When Garrett and Brant heard about it, they offered to do the concert and donate all profits to my shelter. And when Kendra picked up Charcoal last week, she decided not to charge me for her photography services."

"She must have been happy to get her cat back."

"She was. I can't believe he wandered this far."

"There's no telling where tomcats wander."

"Yeah, but he's neutered. Usually that tames them a bit and they stick closer to home. He's never wandered so far before." She frowned. "I'm just glad he ended up here. Her kids were really happy to get him back."

"Sounds like a great opportunity. Getting all those people here will advertise the shelter and maybe drum up adoptions." He drove the final nail into the frame.

"I'm just standing here rattling, while you work. What can I do?"

"No, you weren't. You were helping me hold the frame." He pointed to a bale of hay. "There's a pack of black Magic Markers over there. The float I saw on the net had lines drawn across the cardboard so it looked like slats of wood. Maybe you could make it look like there's wood grain."

"I'll try." She grabbed the markers and an uncut piece of cardboard to use as a guide and got busy. But after a few lines, she set down the marker. "I've got a better idea. Let me run to the house and see if I can find some wood-grain contact paper."

"What's that?"

"It's adhesive shelf liner. Comes in a long roll."

"Who knew?"

"Apparently not bachelors. I donated it for our church's Vacation Bible School last summer and had several rolls left over." She hurried out of the barn, taking her scent with her. "I'll be right back," she called.

An emptiness filled his chest as she disappeared. As if he missed her. And she'd be gone only a few minutes or so.

He was getting way too used to having her around. If only he could tell her how he felt. If only he could plan a future with her. If only he had a future to plan.

Should he have the surgery? Risk ending up in a vegetative state? Or keep living so carefully he wasn't really living?

The sweet hay smell permeated the air. Why were barns so peaceful? Peaceful except when Cody was around, anyway.

"Stop," Ally shouted as a huge wrinkle formed.

"What?" Cody stopped unrolling.

"We've got a wrinkle and it's getting crooked. Just stay put while I fix it." She gritted her teeth as she carefully pulled the paper loose, tugged on each side of the crease until it disappeared, then pressed the paper onto the cardboard again. "Don't take any more backing off until I get this part stuck good." On hands and knees, she crawled around smoothing the paper in place.

"It looks a whole lot better than the one I found on the net." Cody slowly began pulling the back off again as she neared him until they reached the edge of the cardboard. "Now what?"

"Does it look straight?" She stood and surveyed the side of the ark they'd just completed.

"I think so."

"I'll make sure it's all stuck good with no wrinkles and you can trim around the edges. Just leave a couple of inches to fold over so it'll stay securely in place." Back on her knees, she crawled the length of the cardboard until spicy aftershave filled her space. She looked up—right into Cody's aloe-colored eyes. Soothing just like the plant, and for the life of her, she couldn't tug her gaze away.

"Am I leaving enough, you think?" The smell of coffee on his breath sent a shiver over her.

Oh, to get a coffee-flavored kiss from Cody.

"The edge. Am I leaving enough?"

Unwillingly, she looked down at his hands. "Yeah, looks good." But not as good as he did.

She crawled in the other direction. They still had to cut the windows in the contact paper, then line a whole other half of an ark, then attach the cardboard to the frame and stack tons of hay in the trailer. And on their first night of working together, he was already way too hard to resist.

Twelve years and he tempted her heart just as much as he had back then. She needed to put it in high gear, get this float done, stop spending time with Cody and pray for him to move it along. Out of her life again.

"Hey, Ally." Lance stepped in the doorway. "I'm heading out."

"See you tomorrow."

"Could I talk to you a minute?"

"Sure." She stood, brushed off the knees of her jeans. "Did the last patient visit go okay?"

"Fine."

So if it wasn't about the clinic, did he want to talk about Mom? The conversation she'd dreaded since seeing them together at Moms on Main. Which was worse—being alone with Cody or discussing her mom with Lance? A toss-up. Straightening her shoulders, she stepped outside.

"I think we need to talk about your mom and me."

The thwack of the staple gun started up in the barn.

"I don't want to have this conversation." Ally leaned against the wall for support.

"We've always worked together really well, but lately you've been stiff, conversation stilted. Seems like it all happened about the time you caught us on our date."

"So it was a date?"

"I care very much for your mother."

Ally covered her face with her hands. "I'm not ready for this."

"Do you want me to back off?"

"I don't know." She drew in a long breath, dropped her hands. "I know I'm being childish. My dad's been gone twelve years. I know Mom is lonely. I know I should be glad she's found a good Christian man, someone I know will treat her right."

"But I'm not your dad. And seeing her with someone else is tough. Probably makes you miss your dad all over again, too." He set his hand on her shoulder. "I don't want to cause you pain, Ally, but if you ask me to back off, I'm not sure I can."

"That would be selfish." She swallowed the lump in her throat. "Just don't hurt her."

"I won't. We okay?"

She nodded.

"Can I go have a cup of coffee with your mom without upsetting you?"

"She'd like that." She forced a smile.

"Me, too." He shot her a wink and turned toward the house.

Ally stayed there a minute, breathing in and out, listening to the birds and the rhythmic clunk of the staple gun echoing from the barn. She headed back inside.

Cody had already cut out the windows and folded the contact paper through the openings and was in the process of stapling the cardboard onto the frame. Maybe this project could be wrapped up quickly.

He stopped, caught her gaze. "You okay?"

"Fine." She rolled her eyes. "I think he wanted my blessing to date my mother."

"Did you give it to him?"

"Sort of."

"Need this?" He patted his shoulder.

"No. I'm good." She grabbed the window guide and started tracing on the other side of the ark.

Cody's eyes might be the color of a soothing aloe vera plant. But instead of healing, if she got too close, he could inflict third-degree burns. On her heart.

Chapter Nine

The dachshund's long body stretched out on the operating table. In dreamland, the little dog lay with his tongue lolled to the side and his mouth braced open, the anesthesia tube in place.

"There it is." Ally gripped the bulge in the dachshund's intestine with gloved hands.

"What is it?" Derek dabbed blood near the incision in the dog's abdomen.

"We're about to see." She slit the engorged intestine and fished out a hard oval object. "A peach pit. Silly boy, you're not supposed to eat that part."

Derek handed her a suture. "Will he be okay?"

"He'll be just fine." She stitched the slit, carefully pressed the intestine back in place, then closed the incision. "He'll feel a lot better when he wakes up. And probably ready to eat. Can you lock up tonight?"

"Sure."

"Thanks. I'm doing my pet visitation at the hospital." She pulled off her gloves and gave Derek final instructions for the patient as the lobby bell dinged. "I'll take care of it."

Her inspector waited in the lobby. Her blood went

cold. Everything should be fine. She was way under limit. "Hello, Mr. Humphries."

"Ms. Curtis. Whenever there's a problem with a clinic, I make a return visit to make sure things have been ironed out."

"Of course. I just finished a surgery. Let me wash up real quick."

"Do you need to wrap things up with the patient?"

"My vet tech is taking care of him."

"Very well."

"I'll introduce you to Derek and you can inspect the clinic. Then I'll take you out to the barn."

"Lead the way." Mr. Humphries followed her to the back.

Derek had already settled the dachshund in a recovery crate and cleaned the surgical table. They should pass this inspection with flying colors, but Ally still held her breath.

"Derek, this is Mr. Humphries. He's our state inspector."

"Nice to meet you, sir."

"Yes. Likewise." Mr. Humphries peered at Derek's certification on the wall underneath Ally's and Lance's licenses.

"Can you show Mr. Humphries around while I go wash up?"

"Sure."

Ally stepped into the bathroom and leaned back against the door. Was there a mess in any of the rooms? Surely not. Mom or Brandy meticulously cleaned after each patient. But they had been busy today with numerous dog and cat vaccinations and then the emergency surgery. Surely Mr. Humphries understood emergencies.

She pulled off her smock and threw it in the washing machine. If only she could just stay in here. She soaped, rinsed and dried her hands, then sucked in a deep breath and went to face the paws patrol.

As Ally exited the bathroom, Derek and Mr. Humphries stepped out of an exam room. The inspector marked something on his clipboard. "Everything looks good here. As usual. I'm ready to see your shelter, Ms. Curtis."

"Of course." She suppressed a relieved sigh and headed for the barn.

The longest walk of her life. Mind blank, she couldn't think of a thing to say.

"Relax, Ms. Curtis. Remember, I'm on your side. You do good work here."

Tears pricked her eyes. "Thank you."

As they entered the barn, Cody was fastening a collar on the golden retriever mix she'd just gotten in a few days ago, with the spaniel mix she'd had awhile already leashed.

"Perfect timing for their walk. They're exactly the guys I need."

"To visit the hospital. That's why I got them ready." Cody rose up, saw Mr. Humphries. His mouth tightened. "Mr...? I'm sorry—I can't remember your name."

"Humphries."

"Yes. Nice to see you again." Mr. Humphries wrote something on his form. "Tell me about your hospital visits, Ms. Curtis."

"A friend came up with the idea earlier this year. I have several volunteers and we take dogs to visit patients at a hospital and a rehabilitation center. The dogs cheer up the patients, and the program advertises my shelter and the pets I have up for adoption."

"Very creative." The inspector smiled. Actually smiled. "How do you decide which dogs to take with you?"

"Unfortunately, not many fit the guidelines. Cats are too unpredictable and I can't take excitable dogs."

"So only the calm dogs get a chance at adoption through the hospital program."

"Not necessarily." She grabbed her photo album. "When I get a new pet in, I take its picture and put it in this album. When they get adopted, I remove their pictures. So if anyone at the hospital or the rehab center shows interest, I have the album to show them in case they're interested in a different breed or a cat."

"Very impressive." He flipped through the album, then handed it back to her and strolled the long line of pens.

His bushy eyebrows lifted. "Is this all you have? Boarders and shelter pets? I must say I'm impressed. I don't believe I've ever seen so many empty cages."

"Thank you. Cody's been volunteering here and he's had some good ideas for publicity. We adopted out several pets at a church carnival."

"I saw something about a pet photography day and a concert." Mr. Humphries made more notes. Hopefully good ones.

"That was Ally's doing." Cody leaned against a pen. "All proceeds will go to her shelter, and hopefully, more pets will find good homes."

"We're also building a float to advertise my adoption program at a local festival and parade next month." She couldn't take the credit for that. "It was Cody's idea."

"Sounds like y'all make a good team. Good job, Ms. Curtis." He wrote something on his clipboard. "Very good promotions. I might mention your methods to other shelters."

"Thank you, sir." She couldn't keep the grin off her face.

"You've earned your rating of above satisfactory. Keep up the good work."

"I will, sir." As the barn door shut behind him, she

sank onto a hay bale to absorb the compliment. "Above satisfactory."

"That's awesome."

"It really is." All her tension melted away. She could just sit here and cry. But she needed to get on with it. As she stood, Cody raised his hand for a high five.

She slapped her palm against his, then pointed at the two dogs he'd leashed. "How did you know I needed these two for my visitation program tonight?"

"One of your volunteers told me. Could I go with you?"

Cody. In her truck. Visiting patients by her side. Not what she had in mind for a relaxing evening. She'd paused long enough that a frown settled between his brows.

"Sure. But why?"

"Like I said, I'm kind of at loose ends."

"What about your ranch and your new job?"

"My foreman keeps the ranch running like a finely oiled machine, and I teach bull riding only three days a week until we get the word out and get more students. My evenings get long and lonely."

Just like hers. "Okay. We better get going."

"The pets are lucky to have you. And the patients. When I was in rehab after my bull wreck, seeing you walk in my room made my day."

Her breath faltered. Not because of her, she reminded herself—because of the dog. Dogs always cheered people up. "Midnight, the black Lab I had that day, was great with patients. He got adopted pretty quickly after that first visit."

"I don't even remember the dog." His eyes locked on hers.

She concentrated on breathing. In and out.

"I mean, it had been so long since I'd seen you, and then poof, there you were."

Oh. Silly. Of course that was what he meant. "Yeah, well, I'm sorry I didn't come sooner. I tend to get caught up with the clinic and the shelter and let everything else slide. Even friends." But she remembered the night of his wreck. Calls back and forth with Caitlyn, waiting to hear if he'd live. Her stomach took a dive at the memories.

"It didn't matter when you came. Just that you came."

Because they were friends. That was all. "Um, we should go. The hospital administrator is expecting us."

"Lead the way."

Heart, stay under control. It was just Cody beside her. In her truck. Her friend. And only that—all he ever wanted to be. All she could let him be.

Every time Cody got near, Ally startled. Why was she so quiet? And jumpy. He walked backward, slowly pulling the backing off the sticky side of the contact-paper roll as Ally bonded it onto the cardboard.

They'd both gone to Wednesday-night Bible study at their respective churches. Church relaxed him. Maybe it keyed Ally up.

As she smoothed the final foot in place and he peeled off the last of the backing, his ringtone started up—"Amarillo by Morning." He took out his phone.

"It's Natalie. I hit her up to do our publicity for the festival." He pushed the button. "Hey, Nat. You in?"

"In on what?" his publicist asked in confusion.

"On helping with publicity for Ally's shelter for the Peanut Festival."

"Oh, that. Sure, I can help. But not what I called about. I have two offers for you."

"Offers?"

Ally looked up from her project.

"Cowtown Coliseum wants to know if you'd be interested in signing on as a backup announcer at their rodeo and you got an offer to be the spokesperson for a tractor company."

If he kept living, he could be a backup announcer. But he couldn't make that promise.

And the spokesperson thing didn't interest him at all. Would probably involve travel.

"I'm not interested in either offer. I'm happy right where I am, owning my ranch and teaching bull riding." And being close to Ally. He held her gaze.

"All right. I'll let them know, and I'll get with you soon about the parade. Will you ask Ally to keep an eye out for our dog? It's the strangest thing—he knows how to open the gate, so we keep a metal fastener ring in the latch. Only a person can open it, so it's like someone let him out."

"That is strange. I hope your dog turns up. Thanks for calling, Nat."

"What about Natalie's dog?" Ally stood and dusted off her knees.

"She thinks somebody let it out of the pen. What kind of dog does she have? An expensive breed?"

"A chocolate Lab. Rusty. Her husband adopted him from me three or four years ago. He's a great dog. I was shocked the first time he showed up here as a pup because he's full-blood. We don't get many of those. I'll watch for him."

"A pet-napper in Aubrey? What is this world coming to?" She stood the cardboard up and folded the edges of the contact paper through the window cutouts. A long pause stretched between them. "So you turned down offers?"

"To be a backup announcer at Cowtown Coliseum and spokesperson for a tractor company."

"Why'd you say no?"

YOUR PARTICIPATION IS REQUESTED!

Dear Reader,

Since you are a lover of our books – we would like to get to know you!

Inside you will find a short Reader's Survey. Sharing your answers with us will help our editorial staff understand who you are and what activities you enjoy.

To thank you for your participation, we would like to send you 2 books and 2 gifts – **ABSOLUTELY FREE!**

Enjoy your gifts with our appreciation,

Pam Powers

**SEE INSIDE
FOR READER'S
SURVEY**

For Your Reading Pleasure...

FREE!

We'll send you 2 books and 2 gifts
ABSOLUTELY FREE
just for completing our Reader's Survey!

YOURS FREE!
*We'll send you two fabulous surprise
gifts absolutely FREE, just for trying
our books!*

◀ If offer card is missing write to: Reader Service, P.O. Box 1867, Buffalo, NY 14240-1867 or visit www.ReaderService.com ◀

BUSINESS REPLY MAIL

FIRST-CLASS MAIL   PERMIT NO. 717   BUFFALO, NY

POSTAGE WILL BE PAID BY ADDRESSEE

READER SERVICE
PO BOX 1867
BUFFALO NY 14240-9952

NO POSTAGE
NECESSARY
IF MAILED
IN THE
UNITED STATES

"I'm content here." *Being near you, for whatever life I have left.*

"Cowtown is only an hour away. And you said your evenings are lonely. That would occupy weekends."

"Maybe I have something else in mind to occupy my time." He shifted his weight from one foot to the other, ventured a glance at her. *Like you.*

"Cody Warren settling down in one place. For good?"

"Things change. People change."

She searched his eyes. Measured him. But he couldn't tell if he measured up.

"By the way, I'm taking Oreo home with me tonight."

"You think you're ready, huh?"

"My knee is a lot more steady since all my exercising on the treadmill. I think Oreo and I are both ready to put down roots."

"He's all yours."

If only she could be all his. A few more days of working on the float and they'd be finished. He needed to find a new excuse to stick close to her.

If he died, who would keep Ally safe from whatever nut was trying to shut her down? Who would keep her from doing stupid things like climbing in pens with cows separated from their babies?

He had to live. But the only way to do that for certain was to have surgery. And the procedure might just finish him off anyway. But maybe he should consider it. A successful operation was his only chance. To stay alive. To plan a future with Ally.

If she'd have anything to do with him.

"Amarillo by Morning"? Ally unwound the leash from around her legs for the fifth time. The poodle she was boarding seemed intent on tripping her up as they rounded the well-worn path around her back field. All her volunteers had left for the evening. And she was about to wrap it up, too. Almost time for the long hot shower she'd dreamed of all day.

Maybe Cody just hadn't gotten around to changing his ringtone. Or maybe he simply liked the song. Or missed the circuit.

But he'd turned down two good offers last night. That had to mean he was thinking about settling down and staying in town. Maybe teaching bull riding would satisfy his adventurous nature. Could he be content in Aubrey? Could he be content with Ally?

The poodle stopped, statue still, looking toward the road. She cowered and scurried behind Ally.

"What's up with you, Trixie?" Ally surveyed the road. A flash of brown. A bark. "Oh, no. Not another stray. Why don't people at least bring y'all to me, instead of dumping?"

She picked the poodle up and headed for the front yard to investigate. A chocolate Lab sniffed her lilac bush.

"Rusty."

The dog wagged his tail and bounded toward her as Trixie quivered in her arms.

"It's okay, Trixie. Rusty won't hurt you." The large dog wagged his entire body as he reached her. Ally sank her fingers into his thick coat, scratching behind his ears. "He's a good boy. What are you doing here, boy? Your family is worried. Let's get you in the barn and call them."

The good-natured dog followed her to the barn. Barks and yips reached a crescendo at the new arrival as Ally settled Trixie back in her kennel.

"Is that Nat's dog?" Cody took a break from cleaning old hay out of one of the larger pens and rested his chin on the pitchfork handle.

"I'm almost certain."

"That's weird." He wiped sweat from his brow with his sleeve. "You've had two pets wander from the other side of Aubrey within a week's time. And Nat said only a person could unlatch Rusty's pen. Someone had to have let him out."

"Maybe they just forgot to put the extra latch in place and he let himself out." She filled a bowl with dog food and another with water, guided Rusty into one of the large boarder kennels and fastened the latch. "You stay in there."

"Or maybe whoever is trying to shut you down is stealing people's pets and bringing them here."

"Why would they do that?"

"Maybe to get you back over limit. Or to make it look like you're the one stealing the pets."

"That's crazy." She perched on a hay bale.

"It is. But I'm beginning to wonder if we're dealing with someone rational."

She face-palmed. "Oh, that makes me feel a lot better."

"I don't want you to feel better. I want you safe. And if you being cautious helps with that, it works for me." Cody returned to his cleaning.

"Did Mitch get anywhere with the prints he found?"

"No. Whoever we're dealing with has no criminal record."

"That's good, isn't it?"

"I guess." Finished with the pen, Cody moved to the next one. "I just wish we could get to the bottom of this. Maybe I'll ask Mitch to check for prints at Kendra's barn and on Nat's gate."

"You really think it's all connected?"

"Have you ever had any pets from the other end of Aubrey show up here?"

"No." Her shoulders slumped. "I just can't imagine anyone going to so much trouble to mess with me."

The barn door opened and Mom stepped inside. "Oh, Cody. I didn't know you were still here."

"Miss Diane." Cody tipped his cowboy hat.

Mom's smile trembled. She clasped and unclasped her hands.

"Is something wrong, Mom?"

"It can wait until you finish."

"You're making me nervous. Just tell me."

"It's nothing really. It's just—Lance and I want you to get to know him better."

"I've worked with the man for two years." Ally tried to keep her tone casual. "I think I know him pretty well."

"We want you to get to know him outside of work—on a personal level." Mom glanced at Cody, then back to Ally. "We were hoping you could join us at his house for lunch after church Sunday. His daughter and her family will be there, too."

Ally's throat closed up. Her desperate gaze went to Cody.

"I know it's a lot, Ally. I know this is hard on you. But it's really important to me. And to Lance. Just think about it. Okay?"

"Sure." The single word was all she could manage.

"Oh, Ally, thank you." Mom gave her a nervous smile and left.

Cody patted his shoulder.

As if drawn by a magnet, Ally rushed into his arms, pressed her face into his muscled chest. "I can't do this."

"Yes. You can." He gave her a squeeze, then rubbed her back in soothing circles. "You're the toughest woman I've ever known."

"I think it's even more serious than I realized. They

want me to meet his daughter. Like we're gonna end up being sisters or something."

"It could happen. Might as well prepare yourself for it."

"Will you come with me? To lunch Sunday? Give me strength not to act like a selfish brat?"

"It would be my pleasure."

"Thanks." She should take a step back now. Disentangle herself from Cody. Put distance between them. But she couldn't move.

Drat. Not only did she need Cody—she loved him. Had for years. How had she let this happen? What would she do if he left again?

Chapter Ten

Cody rested his elbows on the top rail of the metal arena fence as hoofbeats and snorts echoed around him. The mid-September sun warmed his back as the early evening cooled off.

The bull lurched to the right, flinging his student in the air. Cody pressed the button on his stopwatch as David landed in a heap in the dust. The young man got up quickly and dashed to the fence as two pickup men headed off the bull and drove him to the gate.

"That's better." Cody checked his time. "Almost three seconds."

David hung his head. "Less than half of what I need."

"We'll get there. It takes time and practice to work up to eight seconds." All Cody had to do was get the twenty-year-old past his fear. If David could relax in the saddle, he'd achieve his dream. "Just be patient."

Gravel crunched in the drive behind him. Cody turned. A white truck neared the exit. It had to be Ally. No one else in Aubrey drove a truck with the distinctive mobile-clinic box in the bed.

"My hour's up." David climbed the fence.

"Don't worry—we'll get it. See you Monday."

"Thanks." The teen headed for his truck.

Cody pulled out his phone and jabbed in Ally's number. "Hello?"

"Am I watching you pull out of famous singer Garrett Steele's driveway?"

"Where are you? I mean—I have no idea where Garrett Steele lives. And if I did, I wouldn't tell anyone."

"Uh-huh. Well I'll let you in on a little secret. I teach bull riding at his private ranch. Why don't you come over to the big barn to your left and watch me work?"

"I need to get back to the clinic."

He glanced at his watch. "It's six o'clock. Don't tell me you have more patients scheduled."

"No. But I need to work on the float."

"We're not working on it tonight. You said you needed to get ready for your big pet photography day tomorrow."

"You're right. So I better get to it."

"I'll help you prepare if you'll come help me out. My student might perform better with an audience." Not exactly true, since David had already said his goodbyes. But Cody wanted to see her. Again.

Silence ticked past in seconds. "Okay. But I can't stay long."

The line went dead. Cody's heartbeat filled the silence.

David was almost to his truck. The chute boss swapped stories with the two pickup men still on horseback.

"Hey, guys, can you stick around for one more?"

They looked at each other. Then all three nodded.

"Hey, David, want to go one more round?"

"My time's up."

"I won't tell if you won't."

"Sure." A wide grin spread across the young man's face and he jogged back to the arena. He neared the chute as

Ally parked in the small lot. "Oh, I see. You need me to help you impress the lady."

"Something like that. Give me your best."

"Yes, sir."

Ally strolled toward him. "Will this give me nightmares?"

"It's about as safe as taking a calf from its mama," he cracked, as the chute boss corralled a fresh bull. Metal clanked against metal as the beast tried to buck in the small space.

Ally reached the fence, stepped onto the first rung beside him and hooked her elbows over the top.

"That's David Morris," Cody whispered. "He took lessons at another school for a year. He should be lasting eight seconds by now. The best he's done so far is almost three in his last ride."

"Why can't he last?"

"He hasn't had me as a teacher for very long." He shot her a cocky grin.

She scoffed.

"Seriously—he's scared."

The bull rammed his horns into the chute. Ally jumped. "I would be, too."

"I have to find a way to get him past the fear."

"Maybe he's right to be afraid. Maybe bull riding isn't what he's supposed to do with his life."

"It's his dream. I have to help him reach his goal. Otherwise he'll have regrets."

"But maybe he has a girlfriend who loves him and he isn't supposed to leave her."

Cody's insides stilled. Was she talking about them?

The chute opened and the bull careened out. Ally's hand clamped on Cody's arm, her nails biting into his biceps.

But David matched the bull's movement, in sync with

each buck, each twist. More fluid and rhythmic than he'd ever been.

Cody eyed his stopwatch. Almost five seconds. "I think he's gonna do it."

The bull did a spin that normally would have lost David, but the young man kept his balance. The buzzer went off.

"He did it." Cody let out a whoop. "You did it."

David bailed off the bull and landed on his feet.

The pickup men herded the bull to the gate as David pumped his fists in the air. "Eight seconds? Really?"

"Eight whole seconds. You did it." Cody grabbed Ally around the waist, pulled her off her perch and spun her around with her back nestled against him. "He did it."

Arms and legs flailing, she laughed as he spun her again, then set her down and held her as she wobbled.

"Thanks for the ride. Now I'm dizzy." She leaned back against him.

"I think I figured out how to make David forget his fear."

"How?"

"Get a pretty girl to watch."

"I better get back." She pulled away, practically ran to her truck.

Had she wanted him to stay all those years ago? Maybe her hypothetical girlfriend for David was just that—hypothetical. Or maybe… But if Ally had wanted him to stay, if she'd had feelings for him, there wasn't a thing he could do about it now.

Not unless he did something about the bubble in his head. And lived to tell about it.

If Cody didn't know better, he'd think Ally was avoiding him. Her volunteers had come, walked and fed the dogs, and left. He'd known she wouldn't take him up on his offer to help her get ready for tomorrow's photography day.

If she wouldn't come to him, he'd go to her. He headed toward the clinic, but his nerve ebbed away as he neared. *Calm down.* Don't let her know how desperate he was to see her. He stepped inside. Orange-scented cleaner heavy in the air.

"May I help you?" Her voice came from the back.

"It's Cody. I meant it when I said I'd lend a hand."

"I figured you'd come over when you got ready." Ally came through the door and stopped behind the counter.

"Hey." His breathing went all funny at the sight of her.

"Derek's wife, Brandy, is helping out tomorrow and several of my volunteers will be here, too."

"What can I do?"

"Maybe just greet people." She wrote something on her schedule. "I was going to have the cat pictures taken in the barn and the dog pictures in the clinic. But the barn is such a better background."

"Can't you have both in the barn?"

"Kendra's bringing her assistant." She swept her thick braid over her shoulder and twirled it around her finger. "With two photographers, things will move more quickly if we set up two clients at a time, one with cats and one with dogs. But I can't have dog pictures taken next to cats. That would be mayhem."

"I see what you're saying." He tapped his chin with his finger. "You could use my barn for the cat pictures."

"I thought of that. But your loft is open. I don't want any of my clients' cats getting spooked from all the barking and escaping out of your loft." She opened a drawer and slid a file into place. "And I can't do the dog pictures in your barn, because that would terrorize your cats."

"I'll board up my loft so we won't have any escapees and the cats can come to my barn."

"That would work. But it's a lot of trouble."

"I don't mind."

"Thank you." She set her hand on his arm, warming him all the way to his booted toes. "Now all I have to do is figure out what to do with the dozen or so families bringing cats and dogs."

"My barn will work for that, too. My cats stay in the loft most of the time. And if the dogs are used to cats, they probably wouldn't bother them anyway."

"You're brilliant." She rubbed her temple. "I think my brain is too tired to think anymore."

"Get some rest. I'll prepare my barn and play greeter tomorrow, and you'll be amazed how smoothly everything goes."

"You may regret that offer. We've had such a great response I probably should have made two days out of it."

"No worries. I'll be here."

"Thank you." She looked at him as if he were a hero.

And he felt like one. Ally's hero. A glow filled his chest. What more could he aspire to?

With Lance and Derek manning the clinic, Ally was free to oversee pet adoptions.

Once Kendra had set up all her equipment in Cody's escape-proof barn, Ally watched as she took pictures of the first families on their schedule.

It was nice to see her friends and clients without their pets being injured or sick. A fun, relaxing day and she'd already adopted out three cats and six dogs.

Today would slam her with lots of happy families. Something in Ally longed for that.

"Call me if you need anything," she said to Kendra.

"I better get back to my barn in case there are any potential adoptive families waiting."

"We're good here." Kendra's flash went off as Ally exited.

Outside in the field behind her house, Garrett Steele and Brant McConnell, superstars of the Christian country music scene, performed a concert.

The event was looking to be a roaring success, and to top things off, the two musicians had pledged to match the proceeds of the concert. She'd have plenty of money for another barn—if she could just buy some of the land Cody was leasing.

The bright sun blinded her as she entered her barn. Cody was cracking jokes as Kendra's assistant got some shots of a family of six with their dog.

Her vision cleared enough for her to make out Caitlyn and Mitch milling about the cages.

"Hey, Caitlyn, I saw y'all on the schedule." But as far as Ally knew, they no longer had any pets.

"We've decided to get a dog."

"Oh, how fun. And thank you so much. I can direct you toward kid-friendly breeds and what to expect, though most of the dogs we have are a mixture. Did you have anything specific in mind?"

"Nothing too big, since Michaela is still small." Mitch held their seven-month-old in his arms.

"House or outside dog?"

"Outside. We have a nice barn and fenced-in area."

"I have a beagle mix and a bulldog mix." She toyed with the end of her braid. "They're great with kids and great with other dogs and other animals."

"I had a beagle when I was a kid. I loved that dog." Mitch's expression went distant, his voice filled with reverence.

"Male or female?" Caitlyn shifted her diaper bag.

"Both. The beagle is female. The bulldog is male. Spayed and neutered and up-to-date on shots."

"Can we see them?"

"Of course. Cody, if you'll get Splotch, I'll get Brutus."

"Brutus?" Caitlyn's eyes widened.

"Don't worry. It has nothing to do with his personality. I call him that because he's so stocky and tough looking, but if you adopt him, you can call him anything you want."

Ally and Cody worked quickly, unlatching the dogs' kennels and leashing them.

"I like the name Brutus." Mitch grinned. "What do you think, Micki?" He set their daughter down with her feet on his, took her hands and walked her toward the dogs.

The little girl squealed. Both dogs wagged their entire bodies.

"Easy." Caitlyn dashed after them.

"Both dogs are very easygoing and patient." Ally laughed. "They love attention."

Mitch guided Michaela's hand, petting the dogs, who sucked up the adoration.

"What do you think?" He caught his wife's eye. "Maybe both—they seem to get along."

"I usually kennel them together for companionship and they've become great friends. The bulldog isn't known for energy, but the beagle gets him going sometimes."

"It'd be a shame to split them up." Caitlyn gave her a hug. "Thanks, Ally. They're perfect."

"I'm so glad." She got the paperwork for both dogs. Minutes later, the family and their new pets were in the middle of a photo session, looking as if they'd been together for years.

As they left, Cody settled on a hay bale. "Why didn't they get the third degree?"

"Because I've known them forever. I know their land is the perfect place for dogs to romp and they both had pets as kids. I already know they'll take excellent care of Splotch and Brutus."

"These animals are very lucky to have you. It's obvious how much you care about finding the perfect home for them."

"They're childlike, incapable of caring for themselves." Her mouth twitched as her eyes welled. "They deserve a good life."

The barn door opened. Her mom stepped inside, her eyes wide. "Um, Ally, you need to come to the clinic."

"What's wrong?" She hurried out with Mom on her heels.

"Lance and Derek haven't arrived yet and all the pens are open in the clinic." Mom's words tumbled out. "I got the patients still recovering from yesterday's surgeries back in the kennels just fine. But the Lewis' cat is on top of the refrigerator and the Gonzaleses' dog won't let her come down. And he's kind of big and scary, so I wasn't sure how to handle him."

As Ally bolted toward the clinic, the barn door clapped. "Ally, need some help?" Cody.

"Yes."

Chewed up magazines and an overturned chair greeted her in the clinic lobby. At least the clinic didn't open until ten on Saturdays. Though her four-legged clientele often got messy, she tried to keep the building clean and her first appointment was prone to show up early. A rumbling growl echoed from the break room followed by several gruff barks.

Samson had always been a sweet Doberman, but what if she got between him and a cat he wanted to attack?

"What should I do?" Mom twisted her hands together.

Dobermans and pit bulls were the only breeds Mom was nervous around.

"If you'll take care of that—" she pointed to the shredded magazines in the floor "—and check for any other disorder throughout the building, I'll handle Samson."

With a relieved sigh, Mom got the broom and disinfectant spray.

The door opened and Ally held her breath.

Cody stepped inside. "What's going on?"

"I'm so glad it's you instead of my first client. All the patients were out of their kennels. Mom took care of it except for a Doberman who has a cat treed on top of my refrigerator."

"A nice Doberman?"

"Usually. But I've never had to get between him and a cat before."

"Do you have a plan?" He followed her into the surgery/recovery room.

"Maybe if we put a kennel up level with the cat, she'll go in. Usually when felines are frightened, they love their crates."

"We'll give it a shot."

Ally grabbed Cinnamon's kennel and Samson's leash. Cody was right behind her as she opened the break room door.

"Hey, Samson, sweet puppy." Ally baby-talked the sleek canine. "You don't want to hurt that precious little kitty. Just think how sad her people would be."

Cody strolled past the dog to the refrigerator, took the kennel and held it up next to the cat.

"Come on, Cinnamon. Get in your crate, girl. You'll be safe. Here, kitty, kitty, kitty."

Desperate, the cat shot into the kennel as Samson let out a series of deep woofs and looked as if he'd take Cody down. But Ally snapped his leash on and held him back with all her might.

Cody set the kennel on the counter. "Let me have the dog." He took the leash from her. "Where do you want him?"

"In the surgery room." She followed him through the adjoining door and coaxed Samson into his cage. "I'd think after tangling with a copperhead, the last thing on your mind would be a cat, you brute." Ally scolded the dog and he hung his head as she fastened the cage door back in place. Crisis averted, she let out a long exhale.

"I'll get Cinnamon." Cody disappeared for a moment, then came back carrying a still-terrified cat.

"It's okay, sweetie." Ally stuck a finger through a hole in the box and stroked the frightened cat. "I won't let that mean old dog get you. And your mommy will come get you soon. Let me check you over and make sure you didn't rip any stitches." Gently she pulled the cat out of the cage and set her on the examining table. Ally used her body as a shield to block the cat's view of Samson.

"She just had surgery?"

"I spayed her yesterday." Ally inspected the stitches on the cat's belly. "Everything looks okay. I'm so sorry you had such a traumatic night. I wonder how long y'all were out."

"Your nemesis obviously came back."

"I thought surely the new locks would do the trick."

"I'll see if Mitch is still here."

"Not until the pet photography thing is over." Her insides twisted. "Please. I don't want everyone wondering why the Texas Rangers are here. And I'll have patients soon."

"Relax." He leaned against the counter, crossed his arms

over his chest, as if reminding her how to settle down. "He'll keep a low profile."

"I guess that'll have to do." She checked her appointments. "Thanks for helping. There's no way I could have gotten the kennel up high enough to reach the cat."

"I just can't believe someone was skulking around here last night and I didn't hear a thing. I promise I've been sleeping with both ears open."

"I didn't hear anything, either. It's not your fault."

"No, but if anyone hurt you, I'd never forgive myself." Her heart shot into triple rhythm.

But he cared for her only as a friend. He'd be upset if she got hurt on his watch. Not because he loved her.

The door opened and Lance strolled in. His jaw went slack when he saw her. "Morning, Ally."

"You missed the excitement. I'm sure Mom will tell you all about it. We better get back to the barn and make sure things run smoothly."

"Nice seeing you, Lance." Cody followed her out.

Cars lined both their drives. Though her shelter was less occupied these days, the cacophony of usual barks reached a fevered pitch with all the activity and extra pets. Hopefully, her clients wouldn't leave before getting their pictures done just to escape the ruckus.

"So how are things with Lance?" Cody fell in stride beside her. "After the talk."

"I try to act natural." She slowed to accommodate his slight limp. "But I fake it. It doesn't feel like anything will ever be normal again, and I'm dreading tomorrow's dinner. I'm twenty-nine, my mother has a boyfriend I work with every day, and I feel like I'm losing her. How childish is that?"

"I think it's perfectly normal. You'll never lose her. It'll be different. But different can be good."

"I can't imagine living here by myself." Her eyes went skyward.

"You're probably getting a little ahead of yourself."

"I don't think so." She hugged herself. "He was still at the house when I went in last night. They were holding hands and the way they were looking at each other..." She closed her eyes. "If he kisses her, I'm not sure if I'll scream, cry or laugh. Maybe all three. Yet the rational part of me knows Mom has been lonely for so long. I want her to be happy and he's a good man."

"Just give yourself time to get used to the idea. And pray about it."

"Pray about it?" She stopped. "Like for them to suddenly get on each other's nerves?"

"Not exactly." He chuckled. "Pray for God to give you peace about their relationship."

"I like my idea better." But how could she begrudge her mother the love of a decent man?

By the time they got to the barn, another family was in the middle of their photo session.

Another happy family.

She'd give anything for Cody to return her feelings. But if he couldn't love her, she shouldn't love him. Yet her traitorous heart refused to listen to reason.

Lance's doorbell played some song Cody couldn't quite put his finger on as Ally's hand quaked in his.

"Relax." He squeezed her fingers. "At least you know Lance. You sat with him during church this morning. And for a lot of Sundays before that. It's not like he's some random man preying on lonely women."

"Thanks. You just gave me a whole new worry." She shot him a grin, and despite her nerves, her eyes sparkled with something he hadn't seen before.

Something he liked. A lot.

The door swung open. A pretty redhead with a toddler clinging to each leg greeted them. "Hi, you must be Ally. Come on in. I'm Erin. This is Zane and this is Zoey."

Ally seemed rooted to the spot. He squeezed her hand again, propelling her forward.

"I'm Cody."

"I'm so glad you could come." Erin pried the children loose and grabbed each by the hand. "Everyone's in the living room. Follow me."

They made slow toddler progress to a room just off the foyer.

"Ally, you made it." Diane sat next to Lance on a cozy love seat.

A blond man relaxed in a recliner.

Cody gave her fingers another squeeze, but she pulled free of his grasp as if she'd just remembered they were holding hands.

"This is Ally and Cody. My husband, Scott. If he'll keep up with our two cling-ons, I'll put ice in the glasses and we'll be ready."

"Come here, rug rats." Scott stood and wrangled the toddlers. He tickled the children, reducing them to giggles, as everyone trailed Erin to the dining room.

Something tugged inside Cody's gut. A pull he'd been feeling for a while now. Being home, seeing all his friends and family happily married with kids made him feel like he was missing out on something. Something with Ally.

Diane and the men settled at the table while Erin and Ally filled the glasses with ice. Lance and Diane sat at the ends, Scott and the twins on one side, leaving Cody with Erin and Ally. Taking the middle seat would be too obvious. He chose a chair next to Diane's end, praying Erin would leave the chair beside him for Ally.

He couldn't take his eyes off her. Forever with Ally sounded good. He could imagine spending the rest of his life with her. Her having his babies.

But did she have any feelings for him? She certainly hadn't resisted their long-ago kiss. And since he'd been back, there'd been a few times when she'd seemed drawn to him. Like the other day while they were working on the float. If he didn't know any better, he'd say she'd wanted to kiss him, too.

Finished with the ice, Erin claimed the chair by her dad, leaving Ally to sit beside Cody. Her elbow brushed his. Stole his breath.

"Sorry." That softness was still in her eyes.

That thing that turned him into a puddle at her feet. Could she have feelings for him, too?

But even if she did, Cody didn't know how long his forever would last. He couldn't pursue Ally. Not unless he had the surgery. And lived.

Surgery was his only chance. And Ally was worth giving it a shot.

Grilled steak, roasted potatoes, green beans and yeast rolls. Yum. Ally's mouth watered over the food. But it wasn't enough to distract her from Cody. Since she'd come to terms with her feelings for him, since he seemed like he might stay, she couldn't seem to stop thinking about him.

Lance prayed over the meal, and chatter filled the air as they passed dishes, filling their plates.

Mom seemed so happy. Happier than Ally had seen her since...since Dad. What right did Ally have to let her conflicted feelings put a damper on her mother's happiness?

"So how long have you and Cody been together?" Erin bumped her elbow.

"We're not." Ally gave a decisive shake of her head. "We're neighbors."

"And friends." Cody cleared his throat.

"We've been friends since high school and now we're neighbors." Ally focused on cutting her steak.

"Oops, my bad." Erin offered an innocent shrug. "Y'all seem so close I just assumed…"

"I think—" Scott wiped potatoes off his son's mouth "—my lovely wife was envisioning a double wedding with y'all and Dad and Diane. Guess it'll have to be a single affair."

Erin's eyes widened.

"Ouch." Scott grimaced. "That was my shin."

Ally's gaze pinged from Mom to Lance. Waiting for her response. "A wedding? Isn't that rushing things a bit?"

"Not really." Mom giggled.

Giggled? Mom giggled? "Y'all are talking about getting married already?"

"Since the cat's out of the bag—" a throb started up in Lance's jaw "—I guess I should ask you for your mother's hand in marriage."

Ally's mouth went numb.

Chapter Eleven

"I think Ally's just surprised." Cody's hand closed over hers under the table, gave her a gentle pat. "I mean, you've only been dating a few weeks."

"We've worked together for two years, ate a lot of lunches together and officially started dating six months ago." Mom blushed.

"Six months?" Ally almost swallowed her tongue. "You hid it from me?"

Mom's face went a deeper shade of red. "Um… I haven't exactly been going to book club meetings."

How could she have been so naive? Book clubs didn't meet on Saturday nights.

"Your mother didn't want you to be upset." Lance's tone was cajoling.

"So you hide your relationship from me for six months and then spring a proposal on me out of the blue. What am I? A child?" The high-pitched panic in her voice made her sound like one. She gulped her sweet tea.

Something beeped in the kitchen.

"Ally, let's go check on my pie." Erin scooted her chair back. "I need a second opinion since I'm bad about under-baking the crust and there's nothing worse than doughy pie."

Saved by the buzzer. But the last thing Ally wanted to do was talk about pie. She wanted to grab Mom by the shoulders and shake some sense into her. Instead she pushed her chair back and followed Erin to the kitchen.

"I tried to get them to tell you. From the beginning." Erin opened the oven and slid out the rack. Blueberries bubbled under the golden lattice crust. With mitt-covered hands, Erin pulled the pie from the oven and set it on a hot pad on the counter.

"So you knew they were dating from the beginning?"

"Yes. Dad told me he wanted to ask your mom out and I kind of coached him along."

"Why did they tell you and not me?" Ally folded her arms over her chest as something heavy sank to the pit of her stomach.

"I guess they knew I was ready. I'd been trying to get Dad to date for at least a year."

"But they thought I needed to be treated with kid gloves?"

"I'm married with a family of my own. Your mom didn't want you to feel like she was abandoning you. But it doesn't look like you're alone. Are you sure you and Cody are only friends and neighbors?"

"Yes." Sort of.

Her mom entered the kitchen then wearing a sheepish grin. "How's the pie coming?"

"I think it turned out perfect. For the first time ever." Erin grabbed a knife and the pie and headed for the dining room. "Will you bring the ice cream, Diane? No rush—this'll need time to cool."

"I'm sorry, sweetie." Mom cupped Ally's cheek when they were alone. "I know this must seem fast to you. And

I handled it all wrong. I should have told you from the beginning. Lance tried to get me to."

"Why didn't you?"

"You were so crazy about your dad and I knew it would be hard on you to see me with another man."

"I'm an adult." She swallowed hard. "I'm trying to pull up my big-girl boots."

"We shouldn't have rushed you. Forget about Lance's proposal." Mom patted her arm. "We'll wait until you're more comfortable with everything."

"You really love him?"

"I do. He makes me happy." Mom chuckled. "He makes me laugh. Makes me feel young."

"You're sure enough to marry him?"

"I am." Mom bit her lip. "After your dad died, I didn't think I'd ever love again. But Lance is a very special man. He treats me like a queen."

"You've been alone a long time." Ally drew in a big breath. "You deserve to be happy and Lance is a good man."

"He really is." Mom patted her cheek. "I'm glad you're remembering that you like him."

"We better get back in there with the ice cream."

Mom opened the freezer, fished out the bucket and linked arms with Ally.

They stepped back in the dining room and the conversation went silent.

"Perfect timing." Erin tried to cover the sudden quiet. "I think the pie is cool enough to cut."

"I haven't had blueberry pie in ages." Cody rubbed his hands together.

"It's Mom's favorite." Ally took her seat beside him. "Before we start dishing up the pie, I have something to say."

Lance's jaw tightened. Scott's eyes went big. Erin sipped her tea. Cody's hand found Ally's under the table again.

"I'd like to give Lance my blessing. Yes, you may marry my mother."

Smiles broke out around the table, followed by excited conversation as Erin served up pie and ice cream. Cody squeezed her fingers.

Drat. She'd probably use his shoulder again on the way home. She really should keep her distance. Even if he stayed in Aubrey, he might not have any feelings for her other than friendship. And she wanted way more where Cody was concerned.

"I'm proud of you." Almost home, but Cody wasn't ready to let Ally go just yet. "I know that must have been hard."

"It was." Ally turned into her drive. "But it was the right thing to do. Mom deserves to be happy. And I don't have any right to stand in her way."

"Lance is a good man. And he has no criminal record."

"What?"

Cody ducked his head. "Mitch checked his background after the first break-in at your clinic. He's clean. Derek, too. Of course, I'm not supposed to know any of that, so if you could forget it, I'd be forever in your debt."

"My lips are sealed." She grinned. "Thanks for letting me know, but I already knew he was okay. You can tell a lot about a person from the way they treat animals. His daughter and her family seem nice, too. I could get real attached to those twins."

"You always worried about never being an aunt. Here's your chance." Practice for being a mom to his children someday?

"I hadn't thought of that. But I hope it's a long engagement. I need time to adjust."

"I'll go with you to your mom's wedding if you'll go with me to my grandpa's."

"He's getting remarried?" She killed her engine.

"This Saturday." A chorus of barks from Ally's barn filled the silence. "He called to tell me last night."

"Wow, our relatives move fast, don't they. At his ranch in Medina?"

"It's a six-hour drive. You up for a road trip?" Six hours in a truck with Ally. Could his heart take that much one-on-one with her?

"I guess so. I'll definitely need support at Mom's." She didn't seem to be in any hurry to go inside.

"If we go it alone, you'll have to drive." *Please say yes.* "Or we can ride with my mom and dad in the minivan with my niece, Michaela."

"You know I'm all about kids. But the farther back I sit in a vehicle, the more carsick I get. So I guess I better drive us. How long until you can get behind the wheel?"

He'd hoped she wouldn't ask. Hated lying, but he wasn't ready to share his aneurysm with her. "I'm not sure. Just a precaution because of my knee."

"Isn't that a bit extreme?"

"It was a pretty extreme injury. And not my first." At least that part was true.

"All this time, you haven't driven. How do you get groceries?"

"One of my hands takes care of things for me and takes me where I need to go. And I catch a ride to church with Mitch and Caitlyn."

"That's why you're here, isn't it?" She turned to face him. "Your doctor won't release you to rodeo, either."

"He might eventually. But even if he does, I'm not going back."

"You sure?"

For some reason, his answer seemed to be important to her.

"I'm positive. The rodeo is behind me." It felt good to make plans for the future. Plans with Ally. Monday morning, first thing, he'd call his doctor and schedule his surgery. If he was going to pursue Ally, he needed a guaranteed future.

Sometimes going after what he wanted required a huge risk. Ally was worth the uncertainty.

"Friday?" Ally squeaked. "This Friday?"

"Is it too soon?" Mom winced, set a food bowl in the Rottweiler's cage. "Here you go, girl. You sore, honey?"

Only a day after spaying, the dog looked so forlorn. Ally felt her pain, but give her another day and she'd be feeling better. Maybe Ally would, too. Thankfully the clinic was closed and Ally didn't have any more patients or surgeries after the bomb Mom had just dropped.

"In four days? I just wasn't expecting a wedding quite so soon." Ally went through her closing routine—checking on patients, supplies and her schedule for the next day. But she couldn't focus.

"Well, when you get to be our age, what's the point in waiting?"

"You're fifty-two, Mom. You sound like you're eighty. I just don't understand what the hurry is."

"Lance and I love each other." Mom lifted one shoulder. "We're not silly kids. We want to start our lives together. You're going to Medina Saturday, the Peanut Festival is the week after that, the church is booked the next weekend, and then Erin and her family are going on vacation. It's this Friday or wait a month."

"At least a month would give us a little time to plan—to send out invitations."

"No invitations." Mom held her palms toward Ally. "We both had big weddings the first time. This time we both want small—just our families and closest friends. None of the hoopla."

"Okay." Ally swallowed. "This Friday it is. Tell me what you need me to do."

"Nothing. We're not decorating or having a reception. Just a photographer—I've already booked Kendra—and our families." Mom finished filling bowls and turned to Ally. "The only thing I hate about all of this is you living here alone. With all that's been going on around here."

She hadn't thought of that. After the wedding, Mom would move in with Lance. Ally would be alone.

Mom frowned. "Maybe we should put off the wedding until our mystery is solved here."

Ally wanted to jump on the idea. But more than that, she wanted Mom happy. "No. It could be months before the perp is caught. I'll be fine."

"Maybe Lance should move in with us until things are settled."

"No." Ally's eyes widened. She didn't want to be alone, but she really didn't want to live with Mom and her new husband. "I don't even have to stay here. I can find a new place for my clinic and shelter if you want to sell the house. I need more acreage anyway."

"Nonsense. This is your home." Mom perched on a tall stool. "After all the years I struggled and sold off bits of land to keep this place so you could have it one day, I wouldn't dream of selling it out from under you. But it's yours to do with as you please. If you'd like to sell it and find something with more acreage, you have my blessing."

"I'd like to stay here." It was the only home she'd ever known and her only memories of her dad were here. "As far as the break-ins, Cody's right next door." Though with an excessive number of strays streaming in daily, if the bulk of them didn't turn out to be lost pets, she'd soon be over-limit again.

"Maybe with me out of your hair, you and Cody will get together."

"Mom! We're friends. You know that's all it is."

"I wonder."

"There's nothing to wonder."

"I see the way he looks at you." Mom wagged a finger at her. "The way you look at him."

"We don't look at each other any special way."

"If you say so." Mom hurried toward her desk. "I better get things in order. Lance is taking me out to dinner. Would you like to join us?"

"I'm beat." True. But even if she weren't, she would not be a third wheel. "Y'all have fun."

Mom would live with Lance. And Ally would be alone. Except for her cute cowboy neighbor who rattled her heart.

Ally checked each exam room, wiped down the tables with disinfectant. Where was Cody? She hadn't heard a peep or caught a glimpse of him all day.

Her cell rang and she fished it out. "Hello."

"Hey, Ally." His voice turned her to butter.

"I was just thinking about you." Why had she admitted that?

"Really?"

"I haven't seen you all day."

"Yeah, I was hoping to make it home this evening. But I'm in Dallas. One of my hands and I ran some errands. We couldn't manage everything in one day, so we're getting a hotel room and I won't be home until tomorrow evening."

"Oh." Disappointment loaded her tone.

"I'm having my foreman stay at my house in case there's any trouble."

"Your foreman must be tired of babysitting me."

"Not at all. I'll see you tomorrow evening."

The call ended and she missed him even more.

With Mom gone, would Ally's lonely heart be able to resist Cody?

Aubrey had never looked so good to Cody as Joe drove him through the small town. The leaves hadn't started turning quite yet. Trucks lined Main Street. Suppertime at Moms on Main. His stomach growled, but he wanted to get home.

How had he stayed away for twelve years? After thirty-six hours in Dallas, he was homesick. Mostly for Ally.

But the test his doctor ran yesterday had revealed bad news: the bubble in his head was growing. Finalizing his decision. The week after the Peanut Festival, Cody would go under the knife. His surgeon had explained everything during their consultation that afternoon.

"Lord, get me through this," Cody whispered. "Am I doing the right thing? Just because there's a possible fix for this, am I supposed to try?"

The same peacefulness he'd felt when he first decided to have the surgery flowed through him. For whatever reason, this was the path God wanted for him.

"You say something, boss?" Joe turned onto Cody's road.

"Just praying."

"Didn't mean to interrupt." Joe was still clueless about his health. They'd stayed in a hotel next to the hospital.

While Joe had bought ranch supplies, Cody had walked to the hospital.

His doctor and the internet assured him the surgeon was highly recommended and had performed the procedure successfully countless times. If there had been any mishaps, nobody was telling him.

Even though he might not survive, though he might have a stroke and his reasoning processes or motor skills could be affected, he had to try. For Ally's sake. And with the aneurysm growing, he didn't have much choice anyway. It was all up to God now. Cody could rest in that.

Joe pulled in his drive.

"Thanks for letting me tag along."

"Anytime."

Looked like Ally's clinic was already closed for the day—it was well after five. As he got out of his truck, the door to her clinic opened, and she ran toward him. Right into his arms. It was a dream come true.

With a knowing grin, Joe headed for the barn, made himself scarce.

"We gotta stop meeting like this." The corners of his mouth twitched.

"Mom and Lance are getting married Friday." She sniffled.

"As in this Friday? In three days, Friday?"

She shuddered against him. "It's the only time everybody will be in town unoccupied, and the church isn't available again for a month."

"I'll get you through it. And the next day, you can get me through Grandpa's."

"Why didn't you tell me you were leaving? I was kind of worried about you."

His heart did the two-step. Ally was worried about him. "It came up kind of sudden."

"Is everything okay?"

"It will be." His arms tightened around her. "Everything okay here?"

"Just more strays. And two more escaped pets returned to their grateful owners. I hope there aren't any emergencies this weekend. I'll be in Medina with you, and Lance will be on his honeymoon." She groaned. "With my mother."

Cody chuckled. "At least they're getting hitched and doing it the right way. And as far as the clinic goes, you've alerted the vet in Denton."

"But what if my nemesis decides to pull something this weekend?"

"I arranged for one of my hands to house-sit for you."

She relaxed against him. "Thank you."

"Anything else I can do?"

"You're doing it." She burrowed in closer.

Making his heart clip-clop like a Clydesdale. This surgery had to work. So he could be here for Ally. So he could have the chance to win her heart.

Ally was exhausted. She'd helped her volunteers tend all the animals then had gone to Wednesday-night Bible study.

Though she barely had the energy to put one foot in front of the other after all that, she headed for Cody's barn with a cup of coffee for each of them. She'd have never thought of him as the decaf type.

The usual yaps and barks followed her across the yard. As she neared Cody's barn, something familiar echoed from inside. The nail gun. They'd completed building the frame and contact-papering the cardboard. Only one more night of working together. Tonight they'd assemble the ark, put shelving in place to support a kennel in each window and strategically pile hay bales in the center.

She slid the door open to see Cody holding two sides of the frame together at a right angle.

"Let me help." She set their cups on a hay bale, climbed the ladder next to the trailer and stepped up beside him. As he drove the nail in, she braced her weight against the frame.

"You look tired."

"Thanks. We vaccinated a large ranch today."

"I noticed you were gone all day." He set another nail. "You didn't do anything stupid like get in a pen with a mama cow, did you?"

"Nope. We didn't have any difficult cases. Everyone went right into the chute and took it like a bull."

"I'm glad." He set the final nail.

"Coffee break."

"You speak my language. Decaf?"

"Fake, just for you." She picked up the two cups, handed him his.

They sipped in grateful silence, then set the mugs down and got back to work.

As Cody picked up another piece of the frame and moved it into place, muscles strained against his shirt.

She had to look away as she positioned her foot, hip and hands to hold the frame steady while he sank the nails.

"I did something today."

Like what? Made plans to leave? "What's that?"

"I bought the ranch."

Her breath stilled. "You bought it?"

"I did. And I donated five acres to Ally's Adopt-a-Pet."

His handsome image blurred as hot tears welled in her eyes.

"Now, don't go crying. That's what you wanted, wasn't it? Five acres. I can donate more if you need it. What's five acres or even twenty when I own two hundred fifty?"

"Five is plenty." She blinked several times to clear her vision and braced the frame for him.

He set the last nail, tested the strength of the two curved sides they'd joined together, then stepped back to survey their handiwork.

"Thank you." She flung herself into his arms.

"If I'd have known I was gonna get this kind of thank-you, I'd have bought the land a long time ago." He nuzzled her ear.

Sending a delicious shiver through her. Step back. Better yet, run away. But her boots stayed rooted in place, her body nestled against him. She tipped her head back, looked up at him.

His eyes pledged much more than friendship.

Chapter Twelve

Ally rose up on tiptoe.

His head dipped. Lips met hers. Fireworks went off in her head, heart and veins. Cody filled her senses. The feel of his muscles. The spicy scent of his aftershave mixed with fresh hay. The taste of his fake-coffee-flavored lips. Her hands wound around his neck, fingers curled in his hair.

But then he was pulling away.

She whirled away from him, turned her back to him, tried to get her breathing back on track.

"Ally, we can't—"

"That's twice you've kissed me. Exactly two times too many." Never mind that she'd cuddled up to him like a winter coat on a Labrador Retriever. "Don't let it happen again."

"I was just accepting your thanks." He chuckled.

Her skin went hot. She could only imagine how many shades of red she must be.

"We better get back to work." She closed her eyes, worked at calm and turned to face him. Without looking at him. How could they nonchalantly get on with their day when her whole world had tipped on its axis? Again.

As he held the frame in place and fastened it to the trailer, she braced it for him. He sank nails as if nothing had happened, while she kept her gaze focused on the hay-strewn trailer bed.

"I really appreciate your donation. But you didn't have to do that. I can buy the land from you."

"Nope. It's already done."

He was staying. He'd bought the ranch. So if he was staying, why had he pulled away from her? *"Ally, we can't"* what? Can't kiss? Can't cross the friendship line? Why?

Because he didn't have any feelings for her? Had she misread the message she thought she'd seen in his eyes?

While she was over the moon for him and had laid it all out for him with that kiss. He must know how she felt. And he must feel sorry for her since he didn't feel the same.

Even her toes burned with humiliation.

The dogs were used to his presence. Only the new residents barked their curiosity as Cody finished the pen, tested the latch. Three more pens and he'd feel as if Ally's shelter would be okay if he died.

He'd seen a lawyer after buying the ranch. Arranged for Ally to be his beneficiary. The ranch, his bank accounts, everything. If he didn't make it through the surgery, she'd be able to hire someone to build more pens, another barn, whatever she needed.

But would she have someone to love her the way he did?

Twelve year old memories were hard enough to wrestle with. Revisiting her kiss had kept him up most of the night. He rolled out the fencing and measured for the next pen.

That she had kissed him back must mean she had more than friend feelings for him. But he couldn't do a thing about it. Not until after his surgery. If he survived and still had control of his faculties, then he'd act on it. But not a minute before. His head was fine with that. But his heart was another matter.

Several other volunteers were walking dogs. But no Ally in sight. Maybe she was still at the clinic and he wouldn't run into her. Maybe she was trying to avoid him, too. At this point, space was his best solution. Lots of space between them. And that was doable. They'd finished the float last night.

All he had to do was get through her mom's wedding tomorrow, the road trip to Medina and Grandpa's wedding on Saturday, and the Peanut Festival parade next weekend. Just keep his distance for a little over a week.

The barn door clapped shut and Ally's scent filled the air. "You're building more pens?"

"Now that the float's done, I've got time."

"I'm so excited about the land." She settled on a hay bale beside him. Her knee almost touching his shoulder. "I don't know how I'll ever thank you."

"No need to thank me. I'm just glad to help." His heart skipped a beat. Space. He really needed space.

"I think I'll build another barn with more pens and runs. I have the funds, thanks to the pet photography day and concert."

Chatty. Relaxed. Not afraid to get too close. Not afraid to touch him. Friendly. Like the old Ally.

As if neither of their kisses had ever happened.

Was she on to him? Did she know he was crazy in love with her? Was she trying to remind him of how their friendship was supposed to be? To let him down easy?

"A couple of my ranch hands are starting a construction business. I'll get you their card." The more he could do to help her, the better he'd feel going into surgery.

"Sounds great."

"Ready for the weddings this weekend? And the road trip on Saturday?"

"I'm more at peace with Mom and Lance. They're really great together. Very compatible and happy." She squeezed his shoulder. "You ready for your grandfather's wedding?"

"I'm getting used to the idea. He's been alone about as long as your mom has. No one should be lonely for that long." His throat closed up.

"Project Weddings on track." She stood. Moved away from him. "I better go walk some dogs so my volunteers won't think I'm a slacker. By the way, Mom's wedding will be semiformal. Wear a suit. What about your grandpa's? What should I wear?"

That awesome burgundy dress she'd worn to Landry's almost wedding. Wouldn't mind seeing her in that again. "Casual. Jeans will do."

"That sounds fun. And comfortable."

"Yep." But driving six hours with Ally wouldn't be. How many weddings could he attend with her and keep his distance?

Just get me through ten more days until surgery, Lord. Then with Your help, I'll be a healthy man. And I can eventually see Ally walk the aisle for our own wedding.

All he had to do was survive the surgery with his head, heart and body intact.

The church was pretty as usual. Mom had said no decorations and she'd stuck with it. No extra flowers, no ribbons on the pews, tulle, candelabra or arbors. Just Mom wearing a cream-colored satin jacket and skirt and Lance in a suit, with Pastor William, Erin and her family, Ally and Cody.

The twins were adorable—Zane wearing a miniature suit just like his grandfather's and Zoey in pink ruffles.

These two had Ally wrapped around their little fingers within a mere week.

As her mom pledged her heart to a man who wasn't her father, Ally teared up. Mom was happy and Lance obviously loved her. He'd be good to Mom and she wouldn't be lonely anymore. This was a day for celebrating—even Dad would approve.

"By the power vested in me by the state of Texas, I pronounce you husband and wife. What God hath joined together, let no man put asunder. Lance, you may kiss your bride."

The couple exchanged a chaste kiss, then hugged.

Ally's gaze strayed to Cody and he shot her a wink. Her cheeks went hot. She'd worked at acting natural with him. As if their kiss weren't seared into her memory. As if she had only friend feelings for him. The false front was wearing her out. And tomorrow she had six hours with him in a truck to look forward to.

The gathering took turns congratulating the happy couple and Kendra snapped several pictures of the newlyweds.

"Okay, let's do families, Mom and Ally first." Kendra waved them in front of the altar and took several shots, then some with Lance, too. "Cody, you get in one, too."

"I'm not family."

"No, but you're Ally's date."

"No," Ally squeaked. "We're just friends. Lifelong friends."

"Well, last time I checked, friends can have their picture taken together on special days."

Cody stepped into the shot with Mom and Lance in the middle.

"Now let's do one with the friends, just for fun."

"Good idea." Mom tugged Lance away.

Ally didn't move. Cody didn't, either. Standing there

awkwardly with a gap between them where Mom and Lance had been.

"You'll have to move in closer than that. What? Are y'all afraid of each other?"

They took two steps closer, still not touching.

"Okay." Kendra lowered her camera. "You're friends. So you like each other, right? Act like it! Maybe hold hands. Something not so stiff."

Cody's hand clasped hers.

"That's better." Kendra snapped another shot.

"Will you remember me in a year?" Cody whispered.

What was he getting at? Trying to tell her he was leaving?

"Will you?" He squeezed her hand.

"Yes."

"Will you remember me in a month?"

"I sure hope my memory is that good." She frowned, looked up at him.

"Will you remember me in a week?"

"Duh."

"Knock knock."

Oh. A joke. A relieved grin teased her mouth. "Who's there?"

"See? You forgot me already."

"That's so corny." She giggled, all the tension of the day seeping away. He hugged her close and her hand settled on his chest as they laughed.

"Finally. Now, those were some good shots. Let's get some with everyone. Then we'll do Lance's family."

She'd forgotten all about the camera. The rest of the gathering closed in on them.

"Bride and groom in the middle. Respective families on each side."

After a few pictures, the twins got fidgety. Ally picked

Zoey up and the little girl curled into her. Zane eyed Cody and stretched his arms up, and Cody scooped him up.

Ally bit her lip. He looked good holding a child. Too good. She could imagine marrying Cody. Could imagine them with kids. Could he?

"Very good. Okay, now let's get Lance's family and we'll be done."

Ally and Cody handed the kids over to their parents and settled on a pew to wait. Several minutes later, Kendra wrapped the photo session.

"Thanks so much, Kendra." Ally jumped up to help with her equipment.

"You know how I knew I loved Stetson?" Kendra whispered.

"How?" Why did Kendra feel the need to share this?

"I was all awkward around him. And he made me laugh."

Her gaze cut to Cody talking to Lance. As if sensing her interest, he looked her way. And sent her another wink.

Her cheeks scalded. "We're not—"

"Uh-huh." Kendra slung her bag over her shoulder. "I'll have the pet pictures ready soon. And I hope you'll let me do your wedding photos."

"We're really just friends. Cody makes everybody laugh."

"You just keep telling yourself that." Kendra grinned. "Bye, everyone. I'll get with you about the pictures in a few weeks." She waved and exited the church.

"You sure you'll be all right?" Mom gave Ally a lingering hug.

"I'll be fine. Don't worry about me."

"Comes with the territory." Mom pulled away. "Watch out for my girl, Cody."

"You can count on me."

Then, hand in hand, Mom and her new husband walked out of the church. Leaving Ally behind. Alone.

"You okay?" Cody's calloused hand closed over hers.

She nodded, not trusting herself with words.

"No cleanup. I reckon we can go if you're ready. Best rest up for the trip tomorrow."

"Feel like working on the pens?"

"Sure." His smile lit his eyes as if building pens were his favorite thing to do.

What had she done without him for twelve years? He was such a good guy. Such a good *friend.*

"I need to keep busy." If she went home, with nothing to do, she'd ramble around the empty house missing Mom and drowning in loneliness.

"How 'bout we stop at Moms on Main and get supper."

"Sounds good." She needed Cody today. Not to get too close. But to keep her company. Keep her from being alone. She was almost looking forward to their trip tomorrow.

When had she allowed herself to need him so much?

Once they got on the road, Cody reached for her free hand. Her slender fingers entwined in his. "You're quiet."

"I miss my mommy." Her put-on childlike voice melted his insides.

"Have you heard from her?"

"She called last night—let me know their flight went okay. They're in Florida and the weather is lovely."

"You sleep okay?"

"I cried like a big baby and let both dogs sleep in my bed. I needed cuddling."

He squeezed her hand. "Sorry."

"I'm okay. I'm a big girl. An adult. It just happened so fast. And I never saw it coming."

"It was fast. 'Bout gave me whiplash trying to keep up. I've still got that shoulder if you need it."

"I think I've taken advantage of your shoulder enough as it is. Besides, I'm driving."

Even if he didn't touch her any more than this for the entire trip, he could spend the rest of his days like this. Just being with her was better than any bull ride. Who knew a road trip with Ally would be the highlight of his year? Except for the kiss.

He needed to quit thinking about that or he'd mess up and do it again.

"I just hope none of my clients have emergencies and whoever is out to sabotage me doesn't pull anything."

"You left the vet in Denton's number on your machine. My foreman's staying at my place and Derek and his wife at yours. Besides that, Mitch is keeping an eye on things. And I doubt your nemesis knows we're all gone. Relax."

"I'm trying." She blew out a big breath.

"Why do you always wear your hair like that?" He let go of her fingers, caught the end of her braid and gave it a light tug.

"My hair's so thick and heavy it gets in the way when I'm working."

"But you're not working."

"Habit, I guess."

"Take it down."

"Um, I'm driving. And what, you don't like my braid?"

"I do. But I really like to see it down sometimes. You look more relaxed when it is." He slipped his fingers under the band at the end. "May I?"

"I guess." She rolled her eyes.

He pulled the band free and gently unwound each strand. Fruity shampoo tackled him as wavy tendrils escaped.

"So tell me about the woman marrying your grandpa."

"She's very nice. And she loves him."

"That's all?"

"It's enough." He could barely concentrate. The longing to run his fingers through her silky mane plagued him. He fisted his hand. Stop looking at her. But he couldn't seem to pull his gaze away. Especially with her hair down. "I don't know if you remember or not, but Grandma made quilts."

"I do remember. There were beautiful quilts all over their house when I went to her funeral with you."

"They're still there. When Grandpa asked Vivian to marry him and she agreed, he put all the quilts away so she wouldn't feel like she was moving into another woman's house. But Vivian had a hissy fit. Said such lovely quilts shouldn't be hidden and she wanted to help him keep Grandma's memory alive."

"She sounds great."

"He's been lonely a long time." He really had to stop looking at Ally's delicate profile. He turned away, facing front, leaned back on the headrest. "Like your mom. But we're not losing them. We're gaining new people in our families. New people to love. Speaking of which, you were great with the twins. They sure latched on to you quick."

"It's funny. I've always been better with animals than kids. But those two charmed my boots off."

"I can't imagine having twins." Except maybe with her. With Ally by his side, he could handle anything.

"Definitely double the work." She got quiet again. "But maybe it wouldn't seem like work with the right person at your side."

A comfortable silence settled between them.

Could he be that person for her? Cody relaxed. Content just being with her. How had she woven herself so deeply into his heart?

Chapter Thirteen

Cody snored like a bulldog.

"Wake up. We're here," she said, shaking him a little.

His eyelids fluttered and slowly opened. "We're here? In Medina? You mean I slept the whole way?"

"From the way you were snoring, guess you didn't sleep good last night. Or do you always do that?" She smoothed her hands over her hair, glanced around.

"I don't snore." He looked insulted.

"Got proof." She tapped her phone. A sucking sound echoed from the speaker, then a loud rumble.

"Wow. Are you planning to blackmail me with that?"

"It could come in handy." The homey farmhouse looked the same as it had almost thirteen years ago. Would his family think it odd she was here? Would they assume she and Cody were dating? She'd have to be on guard with her feelings. Especially around Caitlyn. "Did you tell your grandpa I was coming?"

"I mentioned I was bringing a friend. Didn't tell him who." He got out. "I'll get the cases later. Not sure where we'll be sleeping. We may end up in Mitch's cabin."

"You think your grandfather will even remember me?"

She climbed down from the truck. "I mean, he met me during the worst time of his life."

"He liked you. He's even asked about you over the years."

"Really?"

"You're hard to forget."

Her pulse spiked.

The front door opened and Caitlyn stepped out with Michaela snuggled against her shoulder. "Ally. I didn't know you were coming. How did you pry her away from her clinic, Cody?"

"I reckon it was my charm."

"You know, come to think of it, you always could handle her better than anyone else." Caitlyn's suspicious gaze moved from Cody to Ally.

"You make me sound like a donkey or something." Ally hurried to the porch.

"If the hoof fits. But I'm so glad you're here. We'll have so much fun. Just like old times with the three of us back together."

"Let me see that baby girl."

Caitlyn handed Michaela over.

"She's getting so big." Downy coal-colored hair and eyes a vivid blue like her mother's. "And she gets prettier every time I see her."

"Thanks." Caitlyn grinned. "Going on eight months."

"Just wait, punkin." Cody climbed the steps and blew a zerbert on the little girl's fist. "I'm gonna teach you all kinds of things when you get a bit more mobile."

"Don't do us any favors." Caitlyn whacked his shoulder.

"Just a little horseback riding, swimming and fishing. We'll save mountain climbing, hang gliding and bull riding for when she gets older."

"We'll pass on the last three." Caitlyn clutched a hand to her heart.

"Don't even try it." Ally leveled a glare at him.

"Guess I'll tuck my tail and head for the house." He winked at Michaela. "For now."

"Don't worry, baby. Your daddy carries a gun. He'll keep you safe from Uncle Cody's shenanigans." Caitlyn swatted him again as he opened the door for them. "Everyone's gathered in the family room."

The house had changed little from what she remembered of the one time she'd been there.

The scent of the cedar walls gave off a cozy feel as they strolled to the back of the house. In the huge gathering room, Mitch and Grandpa occupied recliners, with Cody's parents, his aunt and his uncle lining the taupe leather sectional.

Tara and a sandy-haired man cuddled in the window seat, and Cody's cousin, his wife and their daughter worked on a puzzle at an oak pedestal table. Three quilts brightened the room.

"Do you know everyone?"

Cody's hand rested at the small of her back. Making it hard for her to think. "I haven't officially met Tara's husband."

"This is Jared. Ally was in the same class as Cody and Caitlyn and owns the shelter where I got Buttercup."

"Nice meeting you," he said.

"You, too. How is Buttercup?"

"We just love her," Tara gushed. "We brought her with us. She's out in the back right now."

"Oh, good. I get to see her."

"Cody didn't tell me his friend was female." Grandpa stood, grasped Ally's hand. "Or have y'all become more than friends?"

"No, Grandpa." Cody's tone was stiff. "We're just friends."

Ally's heart took a nosedive.

Though she had clarified their relationship to others, it hurt to hear it coming from Cody.

"You young people and your issues," Grandpa scoffed. "Silly boy. This girl's much too pretty to be just friends with."

Heat washed over her face. "It's nice to see you again, Mr. Warren."

"Call me Tex."

"Sorry for the teasing, Ally." Mitch chuckled. "It means he likes you."

"I reckon you'll get to meet my bride at the church. I don't get to see her until she walks the aisle." Tex grimaced. "I don't believe in superstition, especially at our age, but Vivian insisted we follow tradition."

"Can I help with decorations or prep?"

"It's done." Audra, Cody's mom, curled her legs up on the couch. "Our crew of ladies was able to come a few days ago."

"What time's the wedding?"

"Seven." Cody checked his watch. "We've got three hours. How 'bout we go for a walk?"

"Look at you raring to go after you slept the whole way while I drove."

"Car rides always knock me out like a light." Cody gave her a sheepish grin. "Maybe a horseback ride would be more relaxing. I can show you the ranch. Unless you're too tired."

"Sounds fun. Lead the way."

As they stepped outside, the late-September afternoon was perfect, the sun warm and bright, with a breeze rustling through brittle leaves. Live oaks with twisted, knobby limbs reached toward the trail on each side of them.

The path beside the ranch house opened into a pasture where a dozen palominos grazed. In the distance, a cabin nestled beside a pond.

"It's beautiful."

"It is. It was hard to leave behind."

"Why didn't you stay here? Why did you come back to Aubrey?"

He shrugged. "Aubrey's home. The bulk of my family is there. And I felt like I was cramping Grandpa's love life here."

So it had nothing to do with her. Not because she'd stumbled upon him in the rehab center with her dog program and he'd realized he couldn't live without her.

"I hope you brought boots."

"They're in my suitcase."

"My kind of gal. Never travel without boots."

If only she could really be his gal.

Cody scanned the church. He'd attended here during childhood visits and his recovery after his bull wreck. Knew several faces but couldn't connect most of them with names. He'd met Vivian's son and daughter and their spouses and kids before the wedding. They all seemed nice. Good Christian people.

This was a positive thing. Grandpa had to be lonely in Medina with the rest of his family in Aubrey. With Vivian, he'd have companionship and he'd still be home.

Ally patted his hand. "You okay?"

Drowning in her coffee-colored eyes, he nodded. How much longer could he resist her? Just another week. Then if he was still alive and still had a brain, wild horses couldn't drag him away.

"I really like Vivian."

"Yeah, me, too. Her husband died five years ago. She and Grandpa have a lot in common."

"I think your grandmother would approve."

"Me, too."

"How come your grandpa lives here and not in Aubrey?"

"This is where the Warrens were originally from. But my uncle Ty traveled the rodeo circuit and met my aunt in Aubrey. After he retired, they settled there and Dad wanted to get into horse ranching. With Aubrey being Horse Country USA, he and Mom decided to make the move."

If they hadn't, he'd have never met Ally. A sinking sensation grew in his gut at the mere thought of not knowing her.

He cleared his throat, kept rambling. "I think they all planned on moving back to Medina, but some of us kids grew up and married locals and Aubrey became home. We tried to get Grandpa to move over the years, but Medina is home to him just as much as Aubrey is home to the rest of us."

Music began and the chatter quieted as the wedding march rang through the church. Grandpa entered from beside the stage and the doors behind them opened as the crowd stood.

Escorted by her son, Vivian wore a denim skirt and red flannel blouse that matched Grandpa's jeans and shirt.

They made it to the altar and her son handed her over to Grandpa. The pastor said a prayer and the congregation sat down. As the vows began, Cody couldn't stop thinking about Ally.

If he lived, complication-free, would she be interested at all? What if he survived surgery and revealed his love for her, and she didn't feel the same? Just because they kissed once—twice—it didn't mean she loved him. Did it?

With a clean bill of health, he could always go back to the circuit. But how empty would that be? Nothing would be the same without Ally. If he made it through the operation and she didn't love him, what would he do? Live next door, humiliated and heartbroken?

He watched her out of the corner of his eye. She dabbed her nose with a tissue—crying over his grandfather's wedding. He had to try.

If she didn't love him, he had to convince her to. For him, there'd been a thin line between the love of a friend and the love of a lifetime. He had to convince Ally to make the leap over the line with him.

Three weddings he'd escorted her to now, and by doggies, the next one would be theirs.

Bleary-eyed, Ally scuffled to the kitchen of Mitch's cabin, drawn by the aroma of freshly brewed coffee. No movement. Someone must have set a timer on the pot last night.

As she neared the couch, she tried to ignore the still form covered in blankets lying there. But as if pulled by a magnet, her gaze darted there.

One socked foot stuck out at the far end. Cody's face was visible. Her steps stalled. He looked vulnerable and a little boyish in sleep. And so handsome.

She could happily wake up to that face every morning for the rest of her life. Stop thinking like that. She shook her head and got moving again.

Focus on something else. The coffee was already made and waiting. She quietly found a cup in the cabinet, poured the fragrant brew and stirred in cream and sugar—careful not to clink her spoon against the porcelain.

Mitch's cabin was all man cave. Unfortunate trophy animals on the walls, antlers everywhere, camouflage galore. A few lavender camo pillows announced Caitlyn's touch.

Quiet. Such a peaceful Sunday morning. Everyone still asleep except her. Mitch, Caitlyn and Michaela in the master bedroom. Though the guest room was cozy, it had taken Ally half the night to relax enough to fall asleep with Cody under the same roof.

"I can't believe it took me this long to catch on," Caitlyn whispered.

Ally jumped, whirled around. "You just took five years off me."

"You're in love with Cody."

Ally's insides stilled. "I am not."

"You are. Don't even try to deny it. I saw the way you looked at him just now."

"I just thought he looked cute. Like a little boy."

"Uh-huh. How long has this been going on?"

"There's nothing going on. We're—"

"Just friends. Yeah, right. Not only are you in love with Cody, but he's in love with you."

"No." Ally pressed a finger to her lips. "He's right there."

"If there's no truth to it, why are you afraid he'll hear? Friends don't get all googly-eyed over each other."

"I've never been googly-eyed in my life and I don't plan on starting now."

"Why fight it?" Caitlyn studied her as if she were a puzzle missing a piece. "I don't understand. You love him. He loves you. Go for it."

"I don't know what you think you saw." Ally tried not to wilt under the scrutiny. "But Cody and I are friends. That's all."

"Mitch and I were high school sweethearts. Everybody expected us to marry after graduation. Do you know why we didn't?"

"No."

"I let fear get the best of me. I don't mean to bring up painful memories, but I was there when you found out your dad had died in the line of duty."

"I remember." Ally tried to swallow the lump in her throat, but it wouldn't budge.

"And Mitch was bound and determined to be a Texas Ranger. I decided I couldn't take the possibility of losing him the way your mom lost your dad."

"I had no idea."

"I let fear keep us apart for ten years." Caitlyn crossed her arms under her chest. "Whatever's holding you back from admitting your feelings for Cody, get over it. Life is short and should be spent with the man you love."

If Caitlyn could see her feelings for Cody, could he? And why did Caitlyn think he loved her back?

"When I meet the man I love, I'll go for it. I promise." The lie tasted bitter. "I better get ready to hit the road." She grabbed her cup and headed for the sanctuary of her room.

"Better get your shower before everyone wakes up. We'll leave for church at ten thirty or so."

"Church?"

"We're all going to Grandpa's church before we leave."

"Oh. I thought we'd head back to Aubrey this morning. But that sounds good." Another lie tumbled right out. Getting entirely too good at this. "I'll be ready."

With Mom not on watch, she'd looked forward to skipping. And now she wanted to escape Caitlyn's perceptiveness as soon as possible.

Besides, she wanted to get home. Back to the safety of sleeping in a whole different house than Cody. The only problem was that getting home would trap her in a truck with him for six hours. Would it be possible to hitch a ride with someone else without raising suspicions? Not with Caitlyn already on to her.

If only Cody could drive. That way she could sleep the whole ride home, since she'd barely slept last night. Maybe he'd sleep most of the trip again.

Movement from the couch.

"Coffee," Cody growled, then sat up, squinted at them and stood. Stiff-legged, he stuck his arms out in front of him like a zombie and lurched to the kitchen.

"Here you go." Caitlyn poured him a cup and handed it to him.

"Mmm." He tilted the mug to his mouth, then jerked away, sloshing the hot liquid over the rim. "Sorry. Is this decaf?"

"One cup of the real stuff won't kill you. And you obviously need it."

He set the mug on the counter, grabbed a soapy dishcloth and wiped the mess from the floor. "Is there another pot? I'll make my own."

Caitlyn sighed. "Go for it, health freak."

How long had he been awake? Had he heard Caitlyn's observations and Ally's denial? And more important, if he'd heard, did he believe Ally's denial?

With her cheeks scalding, she scurried the rest of the way to her room.

As the pastor began to plea for nonbelievers, those struggling with faith issues, or anyone wanting to pray to come forward to the altar call, Ally's breathing constricted. His eyes rested solely on her, as if he could read the struggle inside her.

Pressure in her chest built. Finally, the pastor's attention shifted to another victim. Had Cody or Caitlyn told him she was at an all-time low in the faith department?

No. No one knew. Not even her mom. She was a dedicated pew warmer, there every time the doors were open. And disillusioned every time.

"No, God," she whispered under her breath as the pianist started up. "I do not need You. I let myself need You once and You let me down. Let my dad down. Let my mom down. I don't need You. I don't need anyone. Not even Cody."

Several people went to the altar—including Cody, Caitlyn and Mitch. The faithful, certain God would answer their prayers, thanking Him for the blessings He'd supposedly sent. But Ally wasn't falling for any of it. Not even if her chest exploded.

After four torturous verses, the music faded away and the pastor thanked everyone for coming and called on a man to say the closing prayer.

It was long and flowery and by the time it ended, Ally's teeth were on edge. The amen finally came and she opened her eyes. The congregation moseyed into the aisles, most seemingly in no hurry to get out the doors.

"You okay?" Cody's frown dripped concern.

"Fine. I'm just anxious to get home. Even though Derek assures me everything is fine, with me gone over twenty-four hours, I'm figuring there will be at least fifteen strays and six escaped pets."

"Stop worrying, Suzie Rain Cloud."

"It's the way things have been going lately."

"Can we at least stop and get a bite to eat?" His stomach promptly growled.

Her shoulders slumped. "Sure."

Would this trip never end?

Home for a day. Cody had slept all the way back from Medina even though he'd wanted to enjoy every moment with Ally. But car rides had always made him sleepy unless he drove. Especially without caffeine. Since they'd gotten back, he hadn't seen hide nor hair of Ally.

The float was ready. The weddings were done. What could Cody do now to keep her near once he finished building the pens? He rolled the fencing into place along the frame he'd built. It immediately rolled back up before he could sink a single staple.

It was way after hours. Her volunteers had come and gone. Even though she was shorthanded at the clinic, surely she was finished by now. He dug out his cell, punched in her number.

"*Ally's Veterinary Clinic and Adopt-a-Pet.* May I help you?"

"I'm in your barn slaving over pens for your critters and I could use a pair of extra hands."

Silence. For several seconds. "I'll be right there."

The dial tone started up. Maybe she'd had a rough day without Lance and was just tired.

He had to watch his step with her. Stop giving off mixed signals. Kissing her one minute, keeping her at a distance the next, but not too far. Seven more days.

He'd already come up with an excuse for his impending absence—tests on his shoulder and knee along with ranch errands that could keep him in Dallas for several days. If he woke up in his right mind a week from today, he'd tell her exactly how he felt. And hope she loved him, too.

The barn door opened and she stepped inside, looking defeated.

"Rough day?"

"I'll be glad when Lance gets back. I need him here and I miss my mom."

"You can come over to my house anytime if you need company."

"What do I need to do?" She settled on her knees beside him, dismissing his invitation.

"Just hold the fencing in place while I staple."

"That I can do. Have you heard from your grandpa?"

"They're having the time of their life in Hawaii. I never imagined my grandpa going there."

"We should be glad our loved ones are happy—that they're feeling young and adventurous again." As she crawled on her hands and knees holding the fencing up, her thick braid nearly dragged in the hay on the floor. Her scent and proximity almost overwhelmed him.

He had to refocus on their topic. Oh yeah, being happy for Grandpa and her mom. "I am. It just makes me miss Grandma."

"I know what you mean. I miss my dad. It's like Mom moving on makes me miss him more."

He finished the frame and they went to work on another. Sometimes chatting, sometimes in comfortable silence. Ally was the only woman he'd ever felt completely at ease with without talking. Soon they had the base of the pen and three sides finished. She held them in place while he fired nails with the gun.

"I'll put the door in tomorrow. Want to watch a movie or something?"

"No. I'm tired. Think I'll turn in early."

"Thanks for helping."

"Thanks for building pens for me." She stood. "By the way, they're coming to start the construction of my new barn tomorrow. Garrett Steele and Brant McConnell matched the proceeds from the pet photo day, so I've got funding to cover the entire cost, plus a nice sum left over for pet care and repairs."

Good news. But would she need him anymore? Panic

gnawed at his insides. "Once the barn is up, I can build more pens."

"Thanks. But you've done so much. And there's enough to pay for pens, too."

"But I build them for free. Then you'll have more funds left over for care."

"True." She shrugged. "If you insist."

"See you tomorrow?" He tried not to sound desperate.

"Probably."

One more week. Just one more week.

With Mom gone, Foxy and Wolf vied even more for Ally's attention. Technically, Wolf was Mom's dog. When she came back from her honeymoon, would she take the gray Pomeranian to live with her and Lance? Then Foxy would be as lonely as her person.

A mere three days since Mom's wedding. How would she survive the rest of her life by herself?

She set the dogs off her lap and wandered around the empty house. Both Poms trailed her. Cody's light was on next door. Like a beacon. They'd worked on pens again tonight and again he'd asked her to come over and watch a movie. So tempting. Him and his company.

It was a temptation she could no longer resist. Not after the day she'd had. She hurried to the kitchen, snagged a packet of her favorite microwave butter popcorn and headed for the back door.

"Sorry, guys." She latched the dog gate in place, locking the Poms in the mudroom, and tossed them each a treat. "But I won't be gone long." She grabbed the flashlight and stepped outside.

Barks started up as the door shut. A creepy feeling as if she was being watched washed over her. She shone the light around. Nothing. But all the same, she doubled her speed across the yard and ran up Cody's steps. She'd barely knocked when his door opened.

"Is everything okay?" His hair was wet. Fresh from the shower. Irish Spring soap. Handsome and smelling good.

"I decided to take you up on that movie offer." Maybe this wasn't such a good idea after all. "I brought popcorn."

A wide grin spread over his face. "I'm glad." He took the bag from her. "Have a seat and I'll have this ready in a jiff."

She scanned the room. A dark couch with a recliner at each end. Oreo occupied the one on the right near the remote and a glass of sweet tea sat on the end table.

"Look at you, boy." The dog jumped down to greet her and she scratched behind his ears. "From homeless to a barn, and now you're a bona fide house dog." She settled in the recliner on the left and Oreo hopped up and sat in her lap.

"Traitor." Cody set the bowl of popcorn between them and handed her a glass of swcct tca. "Want me to take him?"

"He's fine."

"You should have brought yours with you." His gazc searched hers. "You sure everything's okay? You were awfully quiet earlier and you just don't seem right."

How did he do that? He'd always known when something was wrong. Her eyes singed. "I had to put a family pet down this afternoon."

He winced, knelt in front of her. "I'm so sorry."

"Me, too." She sniffled. "I never get used to that part of my job."

"Want to talk about it?"

"No." She gave a decisive shake of her head. "I'll turn into a blubbering ninny and that could get messy."

"I can handle it." He patted his shoulder.

"Can we just watch a movie? Please."

He squeezed her hand, then stood, handed her a tissue and crouched in front of the TV. "What movie do you want?" He named off several.

"Nothing where the dog dies." She dabbed her eyes.

"Trust me, I don't have any of those."

Finally, they settled on *Flywheel*. Not only clean but Christian.

"We can have a marathon this week and watch *Facing the Giants*, *Fireproof* and *Courageous*." He sat down in his recliner and looked across at her.

A movie marathon with Cody. Like a married couple, she in her recliner, he in his.

She couldn't think of anything better than this.

When Cody got home from Bible study on Wednesday night, Ally was waiting on his porch with her Pomeranians. Had she even gone? Not unless her church had changed service times.

"Hey. I took them for a walk and came on over since I knew you wouldn't be gone long."

"You didn't go to church tonight?"

She flushed bright red. "My last appointment went late and I couldn't get there in time."

"Come on in." He unlocked the door. "I'll go make the popcorn."

Again they sat on each end of his couch, with her two dogs in her lap and Oreo in his. He'd rather move to the middle. But that would freak her out. And he couldn't let her get that close. Not yet. Maybe tomorrow night he'd go to her house. Fill her empty home with conversation. Get just a bit closer.

"I love these movies." He reached for a handful of popcorn. "They're family friendly and I could watch them over and over."

"I thought I saw a few tears last night," she teased.

"Gets me every time when people turn their lives over to Christ. Even in movies."

She bit her lip, sipped her tea. "Did you see how fast the barn is going up?"

"They'll probably have the frame finished by Saturday." Why didn't she want to talk about Jesus? He knew she went to church, had been a Christian since her youth. But lately she seemed uncomfortable with anything to do with the subject. "So what's the church you attend in Denton like?"

"A lot like the one in Aubrey."

"Do you like it?"

"Sure. The people are nice."

"Okay, but what about the preaching, the worship service?"

She shrugged. "I hadn't really thought about it. I just go with Mom."

"I was wondering since your mom's married now and living in Denton—you'd have to drive to church by yourself. Might be a good time to start coming to Aubrey again."

"We'll see. It's only fifteen minutes." Her gaze never left the TV screen even though he hadn't started the movie yet.

Was Ally in a crisis of faith? Why? And what could he do to help her?

"Better start the movie so we'll have time to watch it all."

He scrutinized her profile a moment longer, then pressed Play. Maybe the Christian movies they were watching would touch a chord with her.

* * *

"Popcorn break." Ally pushed Pause and hurried to the kitchen. For some reason, Cody had suggested they watch *Fireproof* at her house tonight.

"I can't believe how this house looks exactly the same as it did when we were kids." Cody kept his seat on the couch.

"New furniture." She refilled their bowl from the still-warm bag in the microwave.

"Same hardwood floors."

"New walls and paint. A couple of years ago, I decided I couldn't take that old dark, dingy paneling anymore." Back in the living room, she settled on the couch. Put some space between them. "I tore into it with plans for drywall but found this lovely wood underneath."

But Cody scooted her way. "Trying to hog the popcorn?"

Sitting way too close.

Ally's couch didn't have a recliner at each end. She should scoot away, but she pushed Play instead.

As the husband and wife in the movie found their way back to each other, the romance of it moved her. When the main character came to terms with God, a large knot formed in Ally's throat. She closed her eyes, tried to think of something else. Her mind drifted and she yawned.

She'd just rest her eyes and mind. That way God couldn't use the movie to hammer at her.

Mom had forced her to watch the movie before, so she knew how it ended anyway.

Something solid under Ally's head. Solid and it smelled wonderful. Manly cologne.

Huh? She opened her eyes.

Her cheek rested against Cody's shoulder, his head leaning heavily against hers. Level breathing. He was asleep. How could she move away from him without waking him up? Without letting him realize they were basically cud-dling on her couch.

Maybe nice and slow. If she supported his head with her hand, put a pillow in her place.

The TV screen was dark. Dogs barking outside. Please, not her intruder again. But something flickered on the dark screen. A reflection. Like fire. And another scent. Acrid and smoky. Something burning.

She jerked away from Cody.

"What! What's going on?" He blinked several times.

"I think there's a fire." She turned to the window be-hind them, pushed the curtains aside.

Chapter Fourteen

A huge glow. "The new barn's on fire!" *Please God, no.* It was perilously close to the barn housing her strays and boarder pets.

"Call 911." Cody dashed toward the door. "I'll hose down the shelter barn, so it doesn't ignite too."

Ally jabbed the numbers on the phone.

"911. What is your emergency?"

"This is Ally Curtis. My barn is on fire." The operator confirmed the address and Ally hung up, then ran out to help Cody.

He was dousing the front of her stray barn. She grabbed another hose and joined him, though the heat was intense behind them.

Howls and yowls filled the night air. Even if they could keep the second barn from going up, the animals inside were still in danger of inhaling smoke. Though it was completely enclosed, there were pet doors out to the fenced dog runs along each side.

Sirens in the distance. The most glorious sound she'd ever heard. Her throat hurt and she rasped a choking cough.

"Ally, get back. They're almost here and you're taking in smoke." Cody hacked out the last few words.

"I'll go if you will."

He threw down his hose, grabbed her hand. She tugged him toward the barn with the animals as the fire truck with its siren blaring roared into her drive.

"They'll be fine until the fire is under control. If we go in now, we'll only let a bunch of smoke in." He coughed, covered his mouth.

Firefighters spilled from the truck, swarming like ants.

"Anyone inside the structure?" a fireman shouted.

"No. But there's an animal shelter chock-full of dogs and cats in the other barn. We hosed down the side closest to the fire."

They stood back, out of the way as the firefighters rolled out their hose, blasted the fire. An ambulance arrived and soon a paramedic led Ally and Cody to the back, insisting on giving them oxygen.

With the mask strapped in place, Ally breathed deeply. It did feel good. Her lungs eased and the tightness in her throat let up. Within minutes, the fire started to die down.

The paramedic checked them out, removed their oxygen masks.

"Thank you. For saving my animals." Ally flung herself into Cody's arms and soaked his shoulder as all the sobs she'd held back hit her all at once. "Do you think they're okay?"

"I'm sure they are. Don't you hear all that racket? And look—the wind's blowing the smoke away from them. Besides, if any critters inhaled a bit of smoke, I know a great vet who'll fix them right up."

As the flames sizzled into billowing smoke, the fire chief ambled in their direction. "I just called the police in. I'm afraid this fire smacks of arson."

Ally's knees went weak.

But Cody held her up. "Let's get you inside."

"No." She mustered all her strength. "I have to check on the animals."

"Then I'll help you." His arm around her shoulders. "Let's enter through the back door, away from the smoke." He turned to the fire chief. "We'll be in the other barn if anyone needs us."

They rounded the structure. She should move away from him. But she didn't want to.

"I can't believe this," Cody growled.

"You think it's connected with the break-ins?"

"It's too much to be coincidence. This is getting too dangerous." Cody let go of her long enough for her to dig out the key and unlock the door.

Inside, there was only the faint smell of smoke. Thankfully all of the animals seemed fine. Just rattled.

They split up, working each side, strolling along in front of the pens, soothing the boarders and strays.

"Ally." Mitch entered the back door. "You in here?"

"Hi, Mitch." She stopped, turned toward him, slid her hands into her jean pockets.

"Cody, y'all okay?"

"Fine. Just shaken up."

"Did either of you see anything? Hear anything?"

"No." Ally shook her head. "We watched a movie at my house and fell asleep sitting on the couch. I woke up, heard the dogs howling and saw the reflection of the fire in the TV."

"Well, it looks like we've got arson to add to our list." Mitch scribbled something on his pad. "Along with breaking and entering and criminal mischief."

"Great. But it won't do much good until y'all catch this creep." Cody raked a hand through his hair.

"I know it's frustrating, little brother. But we'll get whoever is doing this."

"Thanks for coming, Mitch." She tried to keep her voice even, though her insides quivered.

"I hope you have insurance."

"I do." She hugged herself.

"Good. You'll have to cease construction for a while. It's important the structure stay as is until the arson investigator checks it out."

"She can't afford this setback." Cody grimaced. "After the arson investigator, she'll have to wait for an insurance adjuster before she can get back to barn building."

"Afraid so." Mitch's mouth settled in a firm line. "Unfortunately, it can be a lengthy process."

"Since I can't tell you anything, the fire's out and my animals are okay, I'd love to go to bed." Not to sleep. But to have a good cry before she made a fool of herself on Cody's shoulder again.

"Sure." Mitch gave her an encouraging grin. "You get some rest."

"I'll walk you to your door." Cody fell in stride beside her.

"It's really not necessary." She had to avoid his shoulder and keep herself together.

"It is to me." As they stepped outside, his arm settled around her waist. "Sure you're okay?"

She nodded. "I'm starting to get scared, though. Thank goodness whoever we're dealing with has some semblance of a heart. I'm so thankful it wasn't my shelter barn they set on fire."

"I won't let anything happen to you. Or your animals. If I have to start sleeping during the day and staying awake all night, I will."

"Thanks."

They made it to her door and she couldn't resist one

more hug. She turned into his chest and he wrapped his arms around her.

"Don't worry. I'll keep you out of harm's way."

She did feel safe with him near. Bodily protected. But her heart was a whole other matter.

"I've been thinking." Cody tried to sound nonchalant as he set a kennel in place on a shelf inside the float.

"What's that?" Ally tested the cage for stability and strapped it down.

The sweet smell of hay and peaceful sounds of kittens clambering in his loft couldn't help him. Ally would go into orbit over his idea. "Maybe we shouldn't enter the float in the parade."

"What?"

"Maybe it's too dangerous."

"So you think my nemesis will shoot me off the float in broad daylight?"

Cody's stomach twisted at the thought. "I hadn't really thought that graphically. But I don't think we should risk your well-being."

"The parade is tomorrow. It's a bit late to pull out." She set a larger kennel on a hay bale. "It will give my shelter publicity. And we've worked so hard. We can't let some coward make us quit."

"What makes you think we're dealing with a coward?"

"Someone who creeps around in the wee hours tormenting animals, dumping them and starting fires is a coward in my book." Her tone sounded casual, as if she wasn't worried in the slightest. "Whoever is doing this won't pull anything in public with a crowd."

"What if I ride the float and you stay home?" Maybe he was worried enough for both of them. He'd barely slept last night, jumping at every sound and peering out his window toward her place at least a dozen times.

"I'm going." She checked the stability of the kennel on the hay bale.

"Figured you'd say that."

They worked in silence, setting crates in place. Each kennel had bricks inside to simulate its animal's weight. They'd have to go through the whole routine again tomorrow with actual dogs and cats in the cages. But tonight would ensure there were no mishaps during the parade.

The barn door opened and Mitch stepped inside. "Evening."

Ally jumped, spun around, clasped her hand to her heart. "You just about gave me a heart attack."

So she was shook up. But determined. *Lord, keep her safe.*

"I need to ask you some questions, Ally."

"Sure."

"I know I've asked before, but do you have any enemies?"

"Yeah, whoever's causing mayhem around here."

"Think concrete. Any neighbors complain about your animals? Or clients? Anybody whose pet died in your care?"

"I don't have any neighbors other than Cody. If any of my clients are disgruntled, they haven't told me." Her hand shook as she tested another cage on a high shelf. "And usually they just move on to another vet, not burn my barn down. As far as pets dying in my care, it's part of the job." Sadness tinged her words. "I wish I could save them all, but I'm only human."

"I need you to go through your files." Mitch took down a few notes. "List any clients who haven't brought their pets to you in a while. And any whose pets died in your care."

"My clients are my friends. I can't think of anyone who would pull this nonsense."

"We have to get to the bottom of this." Cody set his hands on her shoulders, forcing her to face him. "Each episode has escalated. We can't sit around and wait until this nut strikes again."

"All right." She sighed. "Once we finish with the float, I'll go through my records."

"I'll be by to get them first thing in the morning." Mitch tipped his hat. "In plenty of time for you to get to the parade."

"Do you think she'll be safe tomorrow?" Cody caught Mitch's gaze, sending him mental pleas to make her stay home. "Should she ride the float?"

"So far our perp has skulked around in the middle of the night. I don't think we'll have any trouble in broad daylight with half the town and countless tourists in attendance."

Mitch didn't play fair.

"That's what I said." Ally quirked an "I told you so" eyebrow at Cody.

"I'm just looking out for you."

His surgery was scheduled for Monday—a mere three days away. He needed Ally safe for completely selfish reasons. So he could tell her how he felt about her.

If he lived. And could still form words.

So far three dog-loaded kennels had snapped into place easily. Now for a cat.

The early-morning sun streaked through the cracks in the old barn as Cody picked up the feline and woofs and yowls reached a fever pitch.

"I know it, boy." Ally soothed a terrier mix as she tested the stability of the kennels he'd already placed—even more carefully than last night since there was live cargo involved. "We'll get moving soon and maybe someone will fall in love with you and take you home."

He wasn't sure about the dog, but Cody was head over heels for Ally. And longed to be her protector until the end of time. Unfortunately, his end of time could come Monday.

For now, he just had to get through the parade. He set the cat's carrier on its designated shelf.

Apparently satisfied with his work, she strapped it down. Her hand grazed his, firing excess wattage straight to his heart. She gave him more of a jolt than any caffeine ever had.

The barn door opened again. "We're home," her mom squealed.

"When did y'all get back?" Ally scrambled down the ladder and Cody hurried to steady it for her.

As Lance entered, the two women hugged.

"Late last night." Diane's smile seemed lit from within.

Happiness was very becoming on her. Cody had never really noticed her beauty before. A lovely older version of Ally.

"I thought you were meeting us at the parade." Ally disentangled herself from her mom.

"We wanted to help with setup." Lance stood awkwardly by. "You don't have to hug me. Unless you want to. I'm just Lance—you don't have to refer to me as your stepdad or anything like that. Unless you want to."

"Welcome home, Lance." Ally gave him a genuine hug, nothing stiff or uncomfortable about it. "I'm glad y'all are back."

"Us, too." He patted her back, obviously grateful for the lack of tension between them. "What can we do to help?"

"Cody will show you while I show Mom. With your help, we'll get this knocked out in no time."

As the foursome worked, yips and yowls intensified while Ally and her mom tried to soothe the disoriented critters. It was refreshing to see Ally so relaxed, in her element and content with her mom's new life.

But he'd rather work with Ally than Lance. Chance bumping elbows with her instead.

Two more days. If everything went well Monday morning, maybe he could arrange to bump elbows with Ally for the rest of his life.

It was so nice to have Mom back. Even though Ally barely had time for a hug before it was time for Lance to drive the truck to the parade with Mom sitting by his side.

The lineup trailed in front of Aubrey Middle School. The Noah's ark float looked great, especially with all the adorable critters peeking through the windows. Barks, yips and meows echoed through the air.

"Wouldn't it be great if you left here today with no animals?" Cody sat on a hay bale between the kennels, not visible from outside the float.

"Let's hope."

A huge banner down the side proclaimed Ally's Adopt-a-Pet—A Noah's Ark of Hope for Homeless Dogs and Cats, along with the phone number. Caitlyn was manning Ally's booth in the field by the old peanut dryer. After the parade, she and Cody would transport the animals to the booth and hope for adoptive families.

He checked his watch. "It's almost time to begin. Guess we should climb up to our perch."

And it hit her. She and Cody would be in close quarters in the elevated platform his ranch hands had built over the gooseneck hitch at the front of the trailer. Putting her above the animals to wave at the crowd seemed like a good idea at the time. But the platform was four by four feet—built for one.

"Ladies first." Cody bowed low.

She turned toward the ladder and he held it steady as she climbed. The platform was nice and sturdy as she stepped up onto it, with railing around the sides except for the entry opening. Attached to the railing, Cody had insisted on two safety harnesses. Side by side, she and Cody would wave at the crowd. As Cody stepped up beside her, the platform seemed to shrink to two by two.

"Buckle up for safety." He wrapped the harness around her waist.

Her breath stopped as he clasped it into place. His hands moved away to his own harness and she started breathing again. Maybe the platform was more like one by one.

Since they were toward the back of the lineup, only a few other floats trailed them, and the horses and horse-drawn buggies brought up the rear. With the slow-moving procession, it would take forever to get to the end of the parade. Stuck on this tiny stage with Cody.

"I think we're starting to move." Cody peered toward the front of the parade.

Several floats ahead of them, she saw movement.

"Be sure and hold on tight when we start rolling."

She gripped the railing, white-knuckled.

"Once you find your balance, then you can wave."

"That's right—you're an authority. You used to ride your horse every year. But I don't remember you riding a float."

"I did once. I happened to be home for a visit and rode the church float a few years back. I didn't hold on good enough, lost my balance and landed in Mrs. Thornbury's lap."

Ally giggled as the vision of him in the ninety-year-old spinster's lap filled her imagination.

The float in front of them inched forward. Seconds later, theirs followed.

"So you must have been glad to see your mom this morning."

"They're ridiculously happy."

"You seem more comfortable with things."

"I'm glad Mom's content and Lance is obviously crazy about her." She shrugged. "How's your grandpa?"

"On cloud nine."

The procession sped up a bit and Ally turned to inspect the kennels below them, making sure none of the animals shifted. The dogs had quieted once they started moving. Probably with their noses sniffing ninety miles an hour at new smells. The cats kept yowling their discontent.

"I know, babies," she called out. "But this bit of discomfort might just find y'all forever homes."

An eternity later, they were finally at the junction to Main Street. As they made the turn, Ally lost her footing.

"Whoa." Cody's arms came around her waist, steadied her, then lingered for a moment.

"It's amazing how wobbly I feel when we're going five miles an hour." She giggled, trying to cover the emotions moving through her.

"You okay?"

She nodded.

"Don't try waving until you're certain you're steady." His hands settled back onto the railing.

And Ally had to concentrate on something else.

Throngs of people lined Aubrey's Main Street. Booths lined the field in front of the old peanut dryer—with people selling crafts, quilts, peanut-themed food and hand-carved items. Every first Saturday in October, the town held the Peanut Festival to celebrate Aubrey's heritage of peanut farms.

Ally let go of the railing with one hand and waved at

the crowd. Lots of people she knew and lots of kids saucer eyed over her dogs and cats.

Her arm bumped Cody's and awareness coursed through her. Oh, would this parade never end?

"I can't believe we adopted them all out already." Cody held his hand up for a high five as Ally drove.

"I know." Excitement sparkled in her voice. "We always get lots of out of towners for the festival. I'm just glad so many wanted pets."

His hand tingled at her brief touch. "Do you ever miss them?"

"I do." Her mouth tilted down a bit. "That's the only part I hate. If I had the time and space, I'd probably keep them all. But it wouldn't be fair to them. Pets need a focused person. Not some crazy lady trying to take care of twenty-five-plus. But knowing they're going to good homes makes it easier."

"You do good work." He found her hand on the console, threaded his fingers through hers. A few more tingles wouldn't hurt. "A lot of those pets are still alive because of you."

"I just wish I could save them all."

"I know." He squeezed her hand as she pulled into his drive.

Movement near her barn caught his attention. The arson inspector?

A man bolted from the barn toward the woods.

"I think we just caught your nemesis." Cody flung the door open.

"You can't go after him." She clutched his hand. "Call Mitch."

"I can't let him get away. You call Mitch."

"What if he has a gun?"

"I'll be careful." He jerked away from her and vaulted out of the truck after the man.

"*Careful* doesn't stop bullets."

Cody's knee throbbed as he ran. But he didn't care. This menace would not get another chance to hurt Ally.

Chapter Fifteen

The man's gait was slow. Cody could take him. Even with his bum knee.

By the time the intruder entered the woods at the back of Ally's property, Cody was almost on him. If he had a weapon, he'd have threatened to use it by now. "Stop. Or I'll take you down."

The man stopped, put his hands up—weapon-free—and turned to face Cody. Gray hair, wrinkled face, kind blue eyes filled with fear.

"Mr. Peters?"

"I didn't do anything. Why are you chasing me?"

Herbert Peters, the man who'd sold Cody his land, wouldn't hurt a fly. "You were at Ally's barn. Were you looking for me?"

"Ally who? I don't know you or any Ally."

"Cody?" Mitch called from a distance.

"Over here. I'm with Herbert Peters."

Footfalls through the woods, and after a bit, he caught sight of Mitch.

"What's going on, Mr. Peters?"

"I don't know. Why are you chasing me? I want to go home." He pressed a shaky hand to his mouth. "I think I left my four-wheeler around here somewhere. But I can't remember where."

"It's okay, Mr. Peters. We'll help you get home." Mitch finally reached them. "You remember me, Mitch Warren?"

"Don't know any Mitch or Warren."

"We all go to the same church. Your wife, Ms. Georgia, was my Sunday-school teacher when I was a kid."

"Mitch. Mitch. Mitch." Herbert tapped his chin with his index finger. "Oh yes, now I remember. You're a policeman."

"Yes, sir, a Texas Ranger."

"I didn't mean to hurt anyone." Herbert shook his head. "I just wanted her to leave. I never could sell my land because of her dogs. Every time I had somebody interested, they'd bail because of those yapping hounds."

"But I bought your land, Mr. Peters." Cody softened his tone, as if he were talking to a child. "Remember? Just a few weeks ago. The dogs don't bother me."

"I don't know you or what you're talking about, son. I just wanted to sell my land, that's all. You understand, don't you?" The old man's gaze went from Cody to Mitch. "Don't you?"

"Of course." Mitch offered his arm to Mr. Peters. "How about I take you home? Your son's probably worried about you."

"I'd be much obliged." Mr. Peters slipped his hand into the crook of Mitch's elbow. "What'd you say your name was again?"

"Mitch Warren."

"Ah, yes. There used to be some Warrens around these parts. You related to them?"

"Wayne and Audra are my parents." Mitch walked the old man out of the woods as Cody followed.

Alzheimer's? Dementia?

"Now, where did you say you're taking me?"

"Home. To your son's house."

"Ah, yes. But what about my four-wheeler?"

"After I get you home, I'll find it and bring it to you."

"That's nice." Mr. Peters patted Mitch's arm. "Such a nice young man. You say I have a son?"

The old man's confusion cracked Cody's heart open.

But at least now Ally would be safe.

"I can't believe it was Mr. Peters." Ally held the Noah's ark frame steady as Cody pulled it apart with a pry bar. "But it makes so much sense. He used to be a locksmith."

"Apparently, he still has lucid moments. He had a few tonight."

"He seemed okay when I talked to him about buying the land." She stared up at the loft window of Cody's barn. The sunset painted lavender, pink and peach streaks across the sky. "Stubborn. But okay."

"He seemed fine when I originally leased the land and then bought it." One side of the frame came loose and Cody set it down on the floor beside the trailer. "His son, Gil, had to sign the paperwork, too—I guess as a precaution."

"I wonder how long he's had Alzheimer's."

"He was diagnosed last year, but I don't think Gil realized how fast it had progressed."

"It's so sad. I wonder what will happen to him."

"He might have to go to court."

She took in a sharp breath. "But I'm not pressing charges."

"You don't have to, since he kind of committed crimes during his nonlucid moments." Cody tore the cardboard off the frame and threw it in a heap by the wall. "But I'm certain a judge will rule him incompetent to stand trial and he'll probably end up in a nursing home."

"I guess he'll be safer that way. It's a wonder he didn't catch himself on fire the other night." She shook her head. "What if my shelter pushed him over the edge?"

"It's not your fault, Ally. He's sick."

She nodded and they worked in silence a few minutes.

They'd already dismantled the platform where they'd stood for the parade and removed all the hay bales. With the frame in four pieces now, Cody got busy prying two-by-fours off the floor of his trailer. His muscles flexed as he worked and she had to look away.

At least they were almost finished.

Minutes later, he threw the wood aside and climbed down the ladder. Taking her hand, he helped her down until her feet touched the barn floor. But he didn't step away.

"I can't tell you how worried I've been about you. I'm glad the mystery is over and you're safe."

"It is a relief. I just wish it hadn't turned out like this."

His tender gaze captured hers and he dipped his head. Their lips met. Her insides curled.

If only Cody had never left Aubrey. Would they have ended up married back then? A lifetime spent with him.

But he had left. Even after their first kiss. He'd left her. And she couldn't let him do it again.

She pulled away, bumped into the ladder behind her.

"Ally, I—"

"Don't." She kept her eyes on the third button of his shirt. "Let me go."

"Ally." His hands fell to his sides and he took a step back.

"If not for your injury, you'd still be on the road refusing to grow up."

"Maybe." He swallowed hard. "But because of my injury, I came back. And I've realized some things."

"Well, bully for you but I won't give up my independence to be your second choice or some sort of temporary detour until you go back on the circuit." She bolted for the door and ran all the way home.

Even though he kept calling her name.

What had he been thinking last night? Cody exited the back door of his barn and strolled toward the feeding troughs, the morning sun warm on his shoulders.

Clearly he hadn't been thinking or he wouldn't have kissed Ally again. He'd gone over and over this. He couldn't pursue her until he survived his surgery. Not a minute before.

Oh, how he'd wanted to follow her home last night. To tell her how he felt. But he couldn't.

Besides, he needed to get to the bottom of her spiritual issues before they could have a relationship. But he'd been so relieved she wasn't in danger. And she'd been so close when he helped her down the ladder. His brain had stalled just long enough for him to kiss her.

He had to concentrate. Feed the calves, take a quick shower, get ready for church, leave Ally alone. Surgery was tomorrow. If he woke up after that, he'd find out where Ally was with God, then tell her everything. Until then, he had to stay away.

"Give me strength, Lord. Strength to stay away from Ally. And give her the wits to draw close to You." He looked up at the clear sky dotted with cotton-ball clouds.

But his head swam. His ears buzzed. Then his vision tunneled. Almost went black. He fell, strewing grain all around him. As his left side hit the ground, all he could think about was how much feed he was wasting. That and Ally.

Had the aneurysm burst? Was this the end? His vision cleared, but he was afraid to move. No pain. So far.

Oreo licked his hand.

"Hey, boy, I think I need help." Where was his cell phone? On the coffee table where he'd left it. "Go get Ally, boy."

The dog kept licking his hand. Guess that only worked with Lassie.

A door shut. Ally. Probably leaving for church in Denton.

"Help! Ally, help!"

Nothing. She'd likely never hear him.

"Help! I'm behind the barn!" *I've fallen and I can't get up.* But it wasn't funny like in that old much-mimicked commercial.

A truck door slammed, followed by an engine starting up. Gravel crunched beneath tires and the engine faded away. She wouldn't be back for at least two and a half hours.

Maybe if he just lay here a minute, the aneurysm wouldn't burst. Maybe then he could make it inside and call for help. But the sky got fuzzy again. His vision tunneled and went black.

As Ally killed her engine, a dog's frantic barking caught her attention. Along with the attention of every dog boarding in her shelter. She jumped out of her truck and bolted toward the barn. But it wasn't coming from there. It sounded like it was behind Cody's barn.

Surely Mr. Peters hadn't evaded his son again. She unlocked the barn and scanned all the kennels. No missing boarders. She darted to her clinic and checked her patients. None missing there either. It must be Oreo.

But he was barking like something was wrong. Maybe he had a loose cow or a snake or a stray cat. She did not want to go over there. After yesterday's kiss, she could never look at Cody again. His truck was in the drive. He ought to be able to hear Oreo and know something was wrong.

Blast, she had him in her contact list. She punched it in. The rings multiplied, then went to voice mail.

She really did not want to go over there. But she couldn't risk Oreo getting snake bitten because she wouldn't swallow her pride and go see about him. She took in a deep breath and trudged toward Cody's barn. As she rounded the back, she could see Oreo barking at something at the other corner. Something wearing jeans and cowboy boots.

Her feet went into high gear. "Cody?"

It was him. Lying on his side.

She reached him and knelt. He was unconscious. She shook him. No response.

"Cody!" His skin was hot. How long had he been here in the dry Texas heat? Thankfully the barn shaded him from direct sunlight.

She jabbed in the numbers on her phone.

"911. What is your emergency?"

"This is Ally Curtis. My neighbor is unconscious."

The operator confirmed her address. "Are you certain he's breathing, ma'am?"

"Yes. I'm a vet." She checked his pulse and respirations, then gave the operator his numbers.

"We'll have an ambulance there as soon as possible. Where are you exactly?"

"We're behind his barn. He lives right next door and we're the only two houses out here."

"Approximately how old is your neighbor, ma'am?"

"Twenty-nine." *Please, God, let him be okay.*

"Does he have any visible wounds or any swelling?"

She scanned his face, arms, hands. "No. He looks fine. I just can't wake him up."

"Does he have any health issues?"

"Not that I know of." A siren whined in the distance. "He did have a bull wreck last spring and his doctor hasn't released him to drive. Because of a knee injury—I think."

"A bull wreck?"

"He was a bull rider in the rodeo. I think he's had several concussions."

"I see."

The siren wailed closer. "The ambulance is almost here. There are two barns here, so I'll go direct them to the right one. Thank you." She hung up.

Hating to leave Cody, she patted Oreo's head. "Good job, boy. You stay with him. I'll get help."

She ran around the barn as the ambulance pulled into her drive. As her heart tried to beat out of her chest, she directed them around to the back of Cody's barn.

The ambulance reversed to him and two paramedics bailed out. "You don't know what happened to him, ma'am?"

"No. I just found him like this. I was gone over two hours, so I'm not sure how long he's been here." Her voice broke. She clamped a hand over her mouth, swallowed hard. "He's hot, so I think he's been here a while. I wouldn't have found him, but his dog wouldn't stop barking. He probably needs fluids."

"Yes ma'am, he does." The paramedics inserted an IV into his hand. "You have medical training?"

"I'm a vet."

"Are you a family member?"

"Um, no. Just a friend. We're neighbors." *And I've been in love with him since I was eighteen years old.* "I need to call his family. What do I tell them?"

"His vitals are stable. Can you do something with the dog?"

"Oreo." She whistled and patted her thighs. "They're helping him. We have to stay out of the way. Come here, boy."

As if he felt guilty for leaving Cody, the dog crept toward her. She wrapped her arms around him.

The paramedics lifted Cody onto a stretcher. "We'll know more when we get to the hospital."

"Where are you taking him?"

"Baylor Emergency. Here in Aubrey."

As they loaded him into the ambulance, Cody's eyes fluttered open.

"Cody! What happened?"

He stared at her a moment, then looked up at the paramedics tending him. "Just got dizzy. I'm okay. Where are y'all taking me?"

"The ER. Just to get you checked over. Now relax, Mr. Warren."

Maybe heatstroke? But it was only in the mid-eighties.

"I'm fine. There's no need for that."

"You were unconscious for quite some time, Mr. Warren. Just enjoy the ride."

She managed a reassuring smile. "Should I call Mitch?"

"No." The word ripped from Cody, his eyes panicky. "I mean, don't worry them."

"I'll follow you."

"I'm fine. It's really not necessary."

Oreo strained against her as if he might leap right into the ambulance.

"I'm okay, boy. I'll be home as soon as they'll let me loose."

The dog settled a bit at the sound of Cody's voice. But as the doors of the ambulance closed and they drove away, Oreo broke free of her grip.

"Here, boy. You can't go with him." She managed to

coax the dog to her side. "Let's put you in the barn so you don't get any ideas, and then I'll go check on him."

Oreo watched the ambulance until it turned onto the street, then followed Ally to her barn.

"I'm sorry to bring back memories for you, but hopefully Cody will be home soon." She put him in his old kennel and poured food in his dish. "Cody will be just fine."

He had to be. If anything happened to him, a piece of her heart would die.

Chapter Sixteen

"We've talked with your surgeon in Dallas, Mr. Warren. We're transporting you there this evening." The doctor checked something on his chart.

"You mean I can't go home?"

"Your surgeon wants to stay on the safe side and keep you in the hospital until your surgery tomorrow."

Cody closed his eyes. "Is my friend still here? Ally Curtis?"

"There was a lady asking about you."

"Can you send her in?"

Something kind and understanding settled in the doctor's knowing gaze. "For a few minutes. Then I need you to rest."

"I promise."

The doctor exited and Cody stared at the ceiling. This was bad. He'd planned to have surgery with no one the wiser. Not Ally. Not his family. He'd written them all letters and left them in envelopes on his kitchen counter—explaining everything—in case he didn't survive tomorrow's surgery. Or in case his brain didn't compute afterward.

But now Ally knew something was wrong. Could he pass it off as heatstroke? Maybe if they'd release him, but not if they were transporting him to Dallas. Besides, Ally was like a bloodhound. She wouldn't rest until she got to the bottom of this.

A knock.

"Come in."

The door opened. She stepped inside, her brows pinched with worry. "How are you feeling?"

"Much better. Like I might live."

"Don't joke. I want the truth. And remember I'm a vet. If I have the slightest inkling you're not telling me everything, I'll call Mitch."

He blew out a big sigh. "Sit down."

She pulled a chair close to his bedside and he clasped her hand in his.

"I have a brain aneurysm."

"What?" Her jaw dropped.

"Probably from too many concussions. After my last bull wreck, rehab and physical therapy, my doctor in Dallas ran a battery of tests and found it. He's not sure how long it's been there."

"What are you thinking? Running a ranch, teaching bull riding?"

"Sometimes they burst. Sometimes they don't. I had a list of triggers to avoid, including caffeine."

Her eyes closed. "The fake coffee makes sense now."

"I couldn't just lie around on my backside and not live because I was afraid of dying."

"So have you had other symptoms?"

"No. Just the dizziness and passing out."

"Aneurysms can cause stroke or death." Her eyes shimmered. "What are they going to do about it?"

"I'm having surgery tomorrow. I set it up a few weeks ago. They're transporting me to Dallas tonight."

"Tell me about the surgery."

"I could die on the table, I could survive with brain damage, I could have a stroke, or I could live and have a normal life."

"I don't want you to die." She laid her forehead against his bed rail. "Or be sick. I can't believe you kept this from me."

"I kept it from everyone." He stroked her hair, savoring the silky feel of it against his calloused fingers. "My family doesn't even know."

She raised her head and her tear-brightened gaze met his. "Why?"

"Because I knew they'd push for me to have the surgery."

"They love you."

"And I love them. But this is my aneurysm, my brain, my life. I wanted to pray and make the decision in peace and on my own."

"Then I'll be there by your side." Her chin trembled. "You can't go through this alone."

"Weren't you steamed at me less than twenty-four hours ago?"

Her cheeks pinkened. "A brain aneurysm puts things in perspective. You have to tell your family."

"Why not just let them be in peaceful ignorance until it's over?"

"And what if you die?" Her voice cracked. "You can't let them be oblivious and then out of the blue die during surgery they don't know you're having."

"Thanks for your confidence in my surgeon." He grinned. When all else failed, crack a joke.

But she didn't smile or laugh. "I'm praying for you to live. But your family needs to know what's going on."

"I left letters for them at my house. If anything happens, you can—"

"Do you want me to call Caitlyn or will you call Mitch?"

She was right. "Can I borrow your phone?" They deserved to know.

"How could he not tell us?" Cody's mom dabbed her eyes with a tissue and his dad gave her a hug.

"He didn't want to worry you." Ally set down the magazine she'd picked up just to keep her hands busy.

"I can't believe he planned to go through this surgery alone." Mitch paced the waiting room.

"If he hadn't passed out and I hadn't found him—" she clasped her hands together to stop their trembling "—he probably wouldn't have told any of us."

"He's so stubborn." Tara leaned into her husband's shoulder. "Always thought he had to do everything on his own."

"Not on his own." Wayne squeezed Audra's hand. "With God. But he still should have told us. I'll give our boy whatfor once this is over."

A nurse stopped in the doorway. "Mr. Warren is prepped for surgery, if y'all would like to see him before they take him back."

Everyone stood. Except Ally. She wanted to see him more than anything. But she wasn't family.

"Come on, Ally." Audra touched her arm.

"You sure? I don't want to get in the way."

"Cody thinks the world of you. There was a time when I thought you might end up being my daughter-in-law."

Her cheeks flushed. "We're just friends."

"Uh-huh." Caitlyn linked arms with Ally and whispered, "Not buying it anymore."

The nurse led them down a long hall, then directed them to a cubicle with the curtain pulled aside. Cody was a bit pale, but other than that, he looked like the picture of health. How could he be so sick and look so great?

"Hey, y'all." He grinned.

Was his perkiness an act for his family?

Audra dabbed her eyes. "I don't know how you can be so upbeat. If you weren't about to go into surgery, I'd box your ears."

"Get in line." Tara sniffled.

"I'll be fine. It's gonna take more than a little blood vessel to take me out." But his eyes weren't quite as lively. He was just as scared as they were. The overconfident bluster was a front.

"I'm glad you're here, Ally." He reached toward her.

She stepped forward, took his hand.

"At least they're not shaving my head."

"Just get well." Her free hand went to his hair as if she had no control and her fingers wound through his waves. "Oreo needs you."

And so do I. Oh, to kiss him. She settled for grazing her lips against his cheek.

"Don't worry." He squeezed her hand. "God's got this."

"He better have." She pulled away and managed a smile. "But I think I'll have a talk with Him just to make sure."

His eyes lit up. "I'm relieved to hear you say that. I was worried you weren't on speaking terms with Him anymore."

"We're good." Or they would be once she did some apologizing. "I'll give you time with your family."

One foot in front of the other, she hurried away before she did something stupid. Like plastering herself against him, begging him to live and love her back.

"I'm going to the chapel." Caitlyn, right behind her. "Want to come with me?"

"Yes." She slowed to let Caitlyn lead.

Just outside the waiting room, she noticed stained-glass windows in paneled doors. She followed Caitlyn inside, where pews lined the large space facing a lit cross.

Caitlyn knelt at the front near the cross. Ally joined her friend there.

Okay, God, I'm sorry for turning my back on You. For pretending I don't need You. When I found Cody unconscious, what did I do? I called out to You—proving that I do need You.

I need You to bless Cody's surgeon's hands. I need You to bless the procedure. I need You to heal Cody. And let him still be Cody. Warped sense of humor and all. Please, let him be healthy and whole.

Waiting for the orderly to roll him into surgery, Cody lay still. If only his brain would stop spinning. What if he had a stroke? What if he couldn't talk or walk? What if he ended up a vegetable?

His parents had gone, along with Tara and Jared, Caitlyn and Ally.

But Mitch stayed by his side. "You okay?"

"So far, so good. I'm kind of hungry, though." Cody patted his empty stomach.

"That's a good sign." Mitch chuckled, but his eyes turned serious. "You should have told us."

"I saved you some worry and myself some pressure while I decided what to do."

"You're right there. Mom wouldn't have let you rest until you scheduled surgery. You scared?"

"Not of dying." His hand shook as he tugged his sheet up against the frigid hospital air-conditioning set on deep freeze as usual. "But living and not being myself, that terrifies me."

"I guess that's why you took so long to decide."

"That and Ally."

"What's Ally got to do with it?"

"I'm head over heels in love with her."

Mitch's mouth twitched. "Tell me something I don't know."

"How?"

"You get all sappy-eyed when you look at her."

"Really?" Cody's grin widened. "Think she knows?"

"Probably not. Women are clueless when it comes to love. You pretty much have to spell it out for them. Put it into words. So you haven't told her?"

"Not yet." Cody closed his eyes. "I decided to have the surgery for a chance with her. But I won't tie her to a vegetable. If everything goes well, I don't have a stroke, I don't have brain damage and I live, I'll tell her."

"What if you have some mild side effect?"

"We'll see. But if I end up half-paralyzed or not knowing who I am or how to speak, I can't saddle her with that."

"Way to think positive, little brother." The seriousness of the situation weighed heavy in Mitch's tone.

"I mean it. If anything bad goes down, I don't want her to know how I feel. Promise me you won't tell her."

"I promise." Mitch patted his knee. "But you'll be fine. We've got all of Aubrey praying for you."

"So much for privacy." Cody rolled his eyes.

The orderly strolled toward them. "They're ready for you, Mr. Warren."

Mitch hugged him. "See you in a few hours, bro."

"I hope so."

Please, Lord, heal me or take me home.

They'd been told the surgery would last three hours. Ally glanced at the clock. Time was almost up. Why wouldn't someone tell them something?

Rubber-soled shoes squeaked on the shiny tile as medical personnel rushed back and forth past the nurses' station.

Mitch paced. Caitlyn flipped through a magazine. Audra and Tara sniffled. Wayne and Jared talked horses, though both were distracted. While Ally slowly went insane.

A nurse stepped in the doorway. Everyone stood.

"Mr. Warren is in recovery. The doctor will be right with you."

What did that mean? In her clinic, it meant everything had gone well and her patient was resting. Ally sank back to her chair. One by one, the others followed. Except Mitch, who continued to pace.

"That means everything's okay? Right?" Audra wiped her nose.

Wayne stroked her hand.

A man wearing blue-green scrubs stepped in the room. "The procedure went well. Everything looks good."

"No brain damage?" Wayne looked like he might fall over.

"There wasn't any bleeding." The doctor's soft tone comforted. "The repair went off without a hitch. We'll know more tomorrow. We'll just have to wait until Cody wakes up."

More waiting. This was torturous.

"How long will that be?" Audra's voice quavered.

"He should be coming out of it soon. He'll probably drift in and out of sleep until tomorrow. We'll see how lucid he is then and run tests. At this point, only time will tell."

But he'd made it through the surgery. With no bleeds. That was a good sign. Every surgery she'd ever done with no bleeds resulted in the pet making a full recovery.

Ally covered her face with her hands. *Thank You, Lord, for letting Cody make it through surgery.*

"Can we see him?" Hope filled Audra's voice.

"Once he's out of recovery, he'll be in ICU. We'll allow two visitors at a time for a few hours and then he'll need to rest. The nurse will let you know as soon as he's in a room."

"When can we take him home?" Ever-optimistic Audra.

"As well as the surgery went, barring complications, usually one to three days."

Meaning Cody could be fine tomorrow. Or he could be a different man.

But he was alive. That was the important part. If he was a different man, they could become friends all over again. If he was a different man, maybe he'd fall in love with her.

Whatever the future held, having Cody alive and well was all that mattered.

Chapter Seventeen

Light. And voices. Cody tried to open his eyes, but they wouldn't seem to budge. Heavy. Heavy eyelids.

He wiggled his toes.

"Hey, I think he's coming around." Mitch's voice.

Surgery. He'd had surgery. And he remembered that. That was good. He smiled.

"What are you dreaming about, bro? It must be good."

He willed himself to open his eyes. It worked this time. Faces came into focus. Mitch and Catherine. No, that wasn't her name. But what was it?

"Hey." She rested her hand on his arm. "How are you feeling?"

"Hungry." His throat was dry, voice croaky. "I want a peanut butter and grape sandwich."

Catherine frowned. But that wasn't her name. "You mean peanut butter and jelly?"

"That's it." Why weren't his words coming out right? Why couldn't he remember his sister-in-law's name? She'd been his friend in school and their youth group long before she'd ever dated his brother. What was her name?

"Lunch should arrive soon. You slept right through breakfast." She picked up a plastic mug of water with a straw, held it to his parched lips. "How about water for now?"

"Thanks." He drank, the iced liquid soothing and cold on his throat. "Am I okay?"

"You seem okay to me."

He focused on her, searching for the right name. "I can't remember your name. I'm coming up with Catherine. But I know that's not right."

Her smile faded. "It's Caitlyn." Sadness tinged her voice.

"That's it. Sorry."

She squeezed his forearm. "They just played around in your brain. I'm sure a little confusion is normal."

"What day is it?"

"Tuesday."

What day had his surgery been? He couldn't remember. "How many days since the surgery?"

"One." Mitch opened the blinds. "You've been in and out. This is the first time you've really been lucid. Must have been some good drugs."

"They got the appendix out of my head?"

Caitlyn giggled. "The aneurysm is gone. They'll run more tests, but your surgeon said everything went textbook perfect and you should get out of here tomorrow or the next day."

Of course. His appendix was in his chest and he hadn't had it since he was fifteen. Why could he remember that, but he couldn't say the right words? Or think them, for that matter. His appendix hadn't been in his chest, but where had it been?

"Only two people can visit you at a time and there are several waiting." Mitch's boots clicked on the floor as he stepped back. "We'll get out of here so you can see Mom and Dad. They've been worried sick."

Was he okay? He had to think really hard. Say the right things. Not worry Mom and Dad.

He had to be okay. Had to have a chance with Ally. Was she one of the visitors waiting?

The nurse checked his monitors.

"Ma'am, can I ask you an answer?"

She cocked her head to the side. "Sure."

"I'm having a hard time coming up with the right talking. Am I okay?"

"I'll have your surgeon speak with you."

Was that a good thing? Would the surgeon tell him his brain was toast?

Ally waited. Everyone had seen Cody. Except her. It was only right. They were family and she wasn't. But impatience gnawed at her stomach. What if the doctor put a halt to visitors before she got to see him?

And she was worried. She'd heard murmurs about Cody saying odd things. Had he had a stroke? His doctor was evaluating him now, then would consult with the family. After that, it was her turn. But what would she find? He hadn't been able to think of Caitlyn's name. Would he even remember her?

Silence reigned among his anxious family members.

Rubber-soled shoes squeaked toward them. Cody's surgeon. He smiled as he stepped in the room. "All of Mr. Warren's tests look excellent. He should be able to go home tomorrow."

"But what about his speech?" The muscle along Wayne's jaw flexed.

"Some confusion in speech is a normal side effect of the procedure Mr. Warren had."

"So he didn't have a stroke?" Audra put into words Ally's greatest fear.

"No. He's doing quite well. His speech should improve over time. It might frustrate him, but he should get back to normal soon."

"So he doesn't have any other side effects?" Mitch sank into his chair. "He's fine. Normal."

"His fine motor skills, mobility and balance are good. All his tests look great. He'll need to take it easy for the next two weeks and no driving. We'll run another MRI and MRA after that and if everything still looks good, he can return to his regular activities. He can even ride bulls if he must."

"Please don't tell him that last bit." Caitlyn squeezed her eyes closed.

The doctor chuckled, then hurried toward the hallway.

Cody was okay. The speech thing was temporary. He could live a normal life.

And go back on the circuit.

"It's your turn to see him, Ally." Caitlyn checked the clock. "Better hurry. Before the doctor decides it's time for Cody to rest."

"I'll wait. He's probably tired."

"I think he'd like to see you." Mitch squeezed her elbow. "I'll show you the way."

How could she say no?

Mitch propelled her down the long corridor. Some sort of alarm started up, sending doctors and nurses scurrying. *Please not Cody.* Her legs noodled.

The staff sprinted into a room. Mitch led her past the turmoil. It wasn't Cody. She started breathing again, said a prayer for the patient in jeopardy. It felt good to pray again.

"He's right here." Mitch gestured to an open doorway, then turned away.

"Aren't you staying?" Did she sound as panicked as she felt?

"I've already seen him. I think he'd like to see you alone."

Ally sucked in a deep breath, slowly let it out and hesitated in his doorway, afraid to enter.

Because she was here only to say goodbye.

"Bye." He waved her inside.

So quick? Her chin wobbled. "You want me to leave?"

"No. Why would you think that?" He stretched his hand toward her. "Please come in."

"You just said bye." She frowned.

He let out a growl. "Don't pay much attention to what I say. I can't seem to get things out right."

"Oh, you meant hello?"

"No. Like what horses eat."

"Hay." She giggled. "Oh, you meant to say hey."

"Even though you seem to think my frustration is funny, you're a sight for sore ears."

Sore eyes? She stifled another laugh. "The doctor talked to you about it. He said it's temporary."

"Yes. But it's very annoying."

"You just got several sentences right." She nibbled on her lip, trying to hold back a grin, but it couldn't be contained and her vision blurred. Only hours ago, she'd thought she might never hear his voice again. So what if he bungled a few words? "And you probably get to go home tomorrow."

"Remember when we were old and we used to hold hands and each waltz a side of the railroad track?"

She chuckled at his slip.

"What did I say?" He rolled his eyes.

"You said when we were old and we waltzed the tracks, but I think you meant when we were young and we walked, unless we've been to Narnia and I don't remember." She flipped her thick braid over her shoulder, twirled the end around her finger. "And I don't know how to waltz."

"Very funny." He reached for her hand.

She shouldn't, but she did. His fingers linked with hers. Warm and strong.

"Anyway, I want to walk the tracks again. And remember how we used to jump from hay bale to hay bale?"

"We had a lot of fun."

"I want to live death to the fullest." He growled. "That wasn't right. But don't tell me. I want to life…life. I want to live life to the fullest. You have no idea how frustrating this is."

"It's temporary, it keeps me on my toes trying to figure out what you're trying to say, and it's kind of cute."

"Cute?" His grin melted her insides.

"I better let you rest."

"I'm too hungry to rest." He held on to her hand. "All they let me have was soup juice and that orange jiggly stuff. I'm dying for a peanut butter and grape sandwich. But they said they didn't have them. And I said it wrong again. Peanut butter and…jelly."

"Very good."

"Ally. There's so much I want to tell you." His tone was thick with whatever was on his mind.

Her heart skipped a beat. "Like what?"

"After I get out of here. When I get better with my talking."

"Okay. We'll talk then." The way he looked at her curled her toes. Had they wiggled something in his brain? Made him have feelings for her?

"I came here not knowing if I'd ever wake up. Now they tell me to take it easy for two weeks and then I can ride buffaloes again."

His slip wasn't funny this time.

She pulled out of his grasp. "How about I go tell them you're still hungry?"

"Stay with me." He reached for her again.

But she couldn't stay a minute longer. "You need food and rest. So you can get well." She backed away, out of the room, and hurried down the hall.

A clean bill of health. And he was already planning to leave.

Thankfully Ally had critters to tend to. A good excuse not to go next door for Cody's homecoming. His family had all left hours ago, except for his mom, who was spending the next few nights with him. There was no reason to go over there. No reason to see Cody for his two weeks of rest. Best to wean herself from his intoxicating presence.

She checked on her patients in recovery one more time, then tested the front door lock and left out the back.

Straight to the barn. She had only four boarders and two strays. The emptiest her barn had been since she started her shelter. And her volunteers had already walked, fed and watered them. She made sure all the runs were open and locked up, then hurried toward her house.

"Ally?"

Cody? What was he doing outside? She turned around.

He stood on his side of the wood rail fence separating their properties.

"Should you be out here?"

"I'm already going stir-crazy. Surely walking twenty feet won't kill me."

"Don't tease like that." Her eyes stung at the memory of finding him unconscious.

"Sorry. Poor word choice." He dug an envelope out of his shirt pocket. "Remember I told you, before I went in the hospital, I wrote each of my family members a letter in case I lived?"

"Why not just tell them what you want to say?"

"I did it again." Cody stomped his foot. "What's the opposite?"

"Oh. You wrote letters in case you—" her throat closed up "—died." Something hard sank to the pit of her stomach at the mere thought of it.

"Yes. I wrote you one, too." He handed her the envelope. Her gaze stayed locked on his.

"Read it."

"Now?" At his nod, she opened the envelope and pulled a single page out.

"Read it out silent."

"Out loud?"

"Isn't that what I said?"

She dragged her eyes from his and concentrated on deciphering his chicken scratch. "'Ally, you've been the best friend I've ever had. I love you and I've arranged for you to inherit my land if I die.'" She clutched her heart. "This is very sweet. But I'm so glad I'm not inheriting your ranch."

"But I've been thinking." He patted the top rail of the fence. "Do you like this wood?"

"Looks like perfectly good wood to me. It's not rotten or anything."

"Not the wood, the hurdle." He gestured at the length of fence between them.

"The fence?"

"That's it. So frustrating." He gritted his teeth. "Do you like this fence?"

"Sure. Are you thinking of building a new one?"

"I think we should tear it down."

"But the fence marks our property lines except for the acreage you donated for my shelter."

He stared up at the sky. "I wanted to wait. To make sure I get the words right. But I can't wait anymore."

"What is it? Are you regretting giving me the five acres? You can have it back."

"I don't want it. The only regret I have is you."

"I'm not following." Did he regret the time they'd spent together in the last month?

"I regret leaving after your dad died. I shouldn't have left you."

"It wasn't your job to stay here and babysit me." She shrugged, swallowed the knot lodged in her throat. "It was hard, but I survived."

"I can't change the past. But what do you think about a corporate takeover?"

"You want to buy me out?"

"No, I want you to be my…partner."

"Oh. A merger." Business partners with Cody? When her heart longed for so much more. "You want to go into business together?"

"Warren Veterinary Clinic/Adopt-a-Pet/Longhorn Ranch."

"You want me to oversee your ranch when you go back on the circuit." Her eyes singed. "My plate's pretty full already. But I'm sure you can find a good manager."

"No." Cody took off his hat and sailed it through the air like a Frisbee. "That's not what I meant. I have no desire to ride buffaloes again. That page of my death is over."

"You're not going back on the circuit?"

"I want you to do the loop with me."

"Do the loop?" Do the loop? Tie the knot? No, he couldn't mean that. Her heart went into overdrive.

"To marry you, Ally. I want to marry you."

His handsome face blurred. "Why?"

"Because." He closed his eyes, concentration apparent in the taut lines of his face. "I love you."

"You do?" Her hand flew to her heart as it tried to beat out of her chest.

"Didn't I say that in my email?" He pointed at the letter she still held.

"I thought you meant as a friend."

"Nothing friendly about it. I've been in love with you since our first kiss."

Tears threatened to spill. "Really?" The word came out barely a whisper.

"If you'd have given me any idea you had the slightest feelings for me, I'd have never left to ride buffaloes. You were never my second choice. Always first. You're my…" His jaw clenched as he searched for the right word. "You're my forever. I hope."

She traced the tense muscles along his cheek with her fingertips. "I love you. I'd love to be your forever. And I'd really love to do the loop with you."

"Really?" His eyes lit up.

"Please tell me this isn't just your scrambled brain talking."

"Nothing scrambled about my feelings for you. How about we seal the deal?" He claimed her lips with a tender kiss.

All rational thought faded away until there was nothing but Cody and the pounding of her heart. She forgot to breathe.

He dragged his mouth away from hers, then leaned his forehead against hers, pulling her as close as he could with the fence between them. "I told you this hurdle was in the way."

Epilogue

Cody's hand shook in Ally's grasp under her mom and Lance's kitchen table. Why was he so nervous? Her mom loved him and he and Lance had built a solid relationship. Though Cody's brain-to-speech issue had completely cleared up in the two months since his surgery, there was no telling what he'd say in his nervousness. He hadn't even touched the four-layer delight her mom had fixed.

It was so old-fashioned anyway. Her mom didn't expect it. Ally should have insisted they skip this step.

Mom popped the last bite of dessert in her mouth, her gaze darting from Ally to Cody and back.

Obviously aware something was up, Lance cleared his throat.

Ally squeezed Cody's trembling hand and he set his tea glass down with a thunk.

"I'm a traditional kind of guy." Cody swallowed hard. "Since Ally's dad can't be here, I need to ask you something, Diane."

"That's what's got you so nervous?" Mom smiled. "I hope it's what I think it is."

"Me, too." Cody drew in a big breath, let it out slow and deliberate. "I'd like permission to marry your daughter."

"That's exactly what I was hoping for." Mom clapped her hands, then stood and rounded the table to Cody's side. "I couldn't ask for a better son-in-law."

"I'm so glad you think so." His hand stopped shaking as he let go of hers. Then he rose and hugged Mom. "I'll take good care of her."

"I know you will." Mom patted his cheek.

"You're not surprised?" Ally couldn't stop smiling.

"Me?" Mom reclaimed her seat. "It's hard to fool a mom."

"Your mother's been onto you since Cody first arrived back in town." Lance smirked.

"How did you know?" Cody took Ally's hand, gently pulled her to her feet and into his arms.

"I knew there was something up between y'all way back." Mom's eyes went to Cody. "But then you left and nothing came of it. As soon as I learned you were our new neighbor, I knew."

"Knew what?" Ally frowned, so certain she'd hidden her feelings.

"I knew there'd be a reunion and sparks would fly." Mom shot her a satisfied wink.

"You hear that?" Cody nestled her close, cheek to cheek. "We got your mom's blessing. We get to tie the knot."

"I can't wait." A contented sigh escaped her. "But I think I'd rather do the loop, if it's all the same to you."

He chuckled, a deep, happy and healthy rumble as his arms tightened around her.

Reuniting with the cowboy of her dreams. She couldn't ask for a better dream come true.

* * * * *

Dear Reader,

Take my theory that the best marriages consist of two people who really like each other, my love for stories about best friends who become more and an old dream of being a vet.

Mix it all together and you get Ally and Cody, a couple who's been running from and denying their feelings for each other for ten years.

Until Cody moved back to town. With a crew of furry friends at stake and still reeling from her dad's death, Ally was determined not to need anyone. Not even God. While she had to overcome her staunch independence to let Cody near, he held a secret that forced him to keep her at arm's length. Cody had to make life-altering decisions, and before Ally could trust him with her heart, she had to learn to trust God again.

Ally and Cody's story is my first friendship-into-romance tale and I think I'm hooked. As an animal lover and rare breed—equally a dog and cat person—the thought of putting a beloved pet to sleep stopped me from pursuing a veterinarian career. Yet I got to live that old dream vicariously through Ally.

I hope you enjoyed reading their story as much I loved writing it. This book launches a new series, so watch for the story of Ally's jilted cousin in the future.

Shannon

COMING NEXT MONTH FROM
Love Inspired®

Available September 20, 2016

THE RANCHER'S TEXAS MATCH
Lone Star Cowboy League: Boys Ranch
by Brenda Minton
Rancher Tanner Barstow knows Macy Swanson is only in Haven, Texas, to claim guardianship of her nephew. But can he convince the city girl to give small-town life—and him—a chance?

LONE STAR DAD
The Buchanons • by Linda Goodnight
Gena Satterfield is surprised when her solitary neighbor Quinn Buchanon starts bonding with her rebellious nephew. He's got a way with the boy—and with her heart—but the secret she's hiding may just tear them apart forever.

LOVING ISAAC
Lancaster County Weddings • by Rebecca Kertz
Isaac Lapp is looking to make amends for the mistakes of his past. Having once abandoned her for the *Englisch* life, can he convince his long-ago friend Ellen Mast of his promise...and of his love?

HOMETOWN HOLIDAY REUNION
Oaks Crossing • by Mia Ross
In town to temporarily run the family business, Cam Stewart begins to reconsider his stay when he reconnects with Erin Kinsley. His best friend's little sister has grown into a lovely woman—one he hopes to make a part of his permanent family.

A TEMPORARY COURTSHIP
Maple Springs • by Jenna Mindel
A chance at a coveted promotion has Darren Zelinsky teaching a class in Bay Willows, where he instantly becomes smitten with Bree Anderson. The charming musician will soon be heading west, unless the hometown boy can show her that her future lies with him.

A FAMILY FOR THE FARMER
by Laurel Blount
Farmer Abel Whitlock is determined to help single mom Emily Elliot run Goosefeather Farm. If she fails, he'll inherit. But he has no interest in claiming the land—he's after claiming his longtime crush's heart.

———————

When Macy Swanson must suddenly raise her young nephew, help comes in the form of single rancher and boys ranch volunteer Tanner Barstow. Can he help her see she's mom—and rural Texas—material?

Read on for a sneak preview of the first book in the
LONE STAR COWBOY LEAGUE: BOYS RANCH
miniseries, THE RANCHER'S TEXAS MATCH
by Brenda Minton.

She leaned back in the seat and covered her face with her hands. "I am angry. I'm mad because I don't know what to do for Colby. And the person I always went to for advice is gone. Grant is gone. I think Colby and I were both in a delusional state, thinking they would come home. But they're not. I'm not getting my brother, my best friend, back. Colby isn't getting his parents back. And it isn't fair. It isn't fair that I had to—"

Her eyes closed, and she shook her head.

"Macy?"

She pinched the bridge of her nose. "No. I'm not going to say that. I lost a job and gave up an apartment. Colby lost his parents. What I lost doesn't amount to anything. I lost things I don't miss."

"I think you're wrong. I think you miss your life. There's nothing wrong with that. Accept it, or it'll eat you up."

Tanner pulled up to her house.

"I miss my life." She said it on a sigh. "I wouldn't be anywhere else. But I have to admit, there are days I wonder if Colby would be better off with someone else, with anyone but me. But I'm his family. We have each other."

"Yes, and in the end, that matters."

"But…" She bit down on her lip and glanced away from him, not finishing.

"But what?"

"What if I'm not a mom? What if I can't do this?" She looked young sitting next to him, her green eyes troubled.

"I'm guessing that even a mom who planned on having a child would still question if she could do it."

She reached for the door. "Thank you for letting me talk about Colby."

"Anytime." He said it, and then he realized the door that had opened.

She laughed. "Don't worry. I won't be calling at midnight to talk about my feelings."

"If you did, I'd answer."

She stood on tiptoe and touched his cheek to bring it down to her level. When she kissed him, he felt floored by the unexpected gesture. Macy had soft hair, soft gestures and a soft heart. She was easy to like. He guessed if a man wasn't careful, he'd find himself falling a little in love with her.

Don't miss
THE RANCHER'S TEXAS MATCH by Brenda Minton,
available October 2016 wherever
Love Inspired® books and ebooks are sold.

www.LoveInspired.com